Phantom Rider

Phantom Rider

Book Five of
The Clint Mason Series

by

William F. Martin

authorHOUSE®

AuthorHouse™
1663 Liberty Drive
Bloomington, IN 47403
www.authorhouse.com
Phone: 1-800-839-8640

Published by AuthorHouse 10/29/2012

ISBN: 978-1-4772-8264-9 (sc)
ISBN: 978-1-4772-8328-8 (e)

Chapter 1

The talkative gambler had no idea of the trouble he was stirring up. While his tale of two families being driven off their ranches by rich land grabbers from St. Louis and Chicago was a common occurrence on the gold coast of California, what this gambler did not know was the amount of personal interest in the families held by one of the listeners.

The lean, tall, olive-skinned cowboy showed no outward signs of the turmoil churning deep within his chest. His stone face masked completely the raging thoughts going through Clint Mason's brain. A very observant gambler may have picked up on a tightening of Clint's jaw muscles, but other than that slight sign, the poker game continued without a change. A more delayed reaction was the steady flow of chips into Clint's stack. The possibility that his two young families had been cheated out of the ranches that Clint had set them up on changed his game. Knowing that his gambling skills were far above this group, he had been playing for pure fun, taking it easy on the other players at the table. His new anger turned against the messenger, even though he knew that was not logical.

It only took an hour or so for the talkative messenger to be wiped out of his table stakes. Clint followed the newly broke gambler to the bar to buy the man a few drinks. The tales of the young

California ranching families continued to pour out of the messenger as Clint kept their glasses full and his ear attentive. The man said that he had been in Sacramento, California, when he first heard the story, almost two months ago. He had joined a table of cards which turned out to be dominated by several poker players from the Starr Ranch, just south of Sacramento, down toward San Francisco. The Starr Ranch cowboys were trading stories with two other players, stories about Senator Crane and the Phillips Freight Company out of St. Louis.

These Starr Ranch cowboys had relayed the story that it was just one gun-slinging gambler who had killed several Starr Ranch cowboys and then taken possession of two cattle and horse ranches from Mr. Starr, their boss. The story did not reveal that the real economic loss to the Starr Enterprise was the lucrative timber contract to the railroad based on these acres of range.

Senator Joseph Crane was a major supporter for the westward extension of the railroads into California. It was also rumored, but had never been proven, that his brother-in-law, Julius Phillips, along with Senator Crane, had made huge fortunes through contracts with the railroad for timber, land and freight. Following that gunfight, the sheriff from San Francisco had identified one of the bodies he found in the streets of Bay Town as that of Charles Martinez, the lone gunman. The top gun hand for the Starr Ranch, John Hayes, left town and was reportedly seen along with his large Appaloosa stallion in Carson City.

The story continued that the Starr Ranch killing of Charles Martinez in Bay Town was a wasted effort because Señor Martinez had already transferred ownership of the two ranches to two ex-Army soldiers and their ranch hands. The storyteller continued that this had all happened almost six months ago. It had taken all this time for the Starr Ranch to recruit new gun hands and renew its quest to own those two timber-rich ranches.

As he listened, Clint's mind went back to his time in San Francisco where he had been known as Charles Martinez. It seemed like years ago, even though it had been less than 12 months since he had set out to buy a ranch to breed top quality horses and cattle, marry and settle down. He had found two ranches side by side that were going broke due to consistent rustling by neighboring Starr Ranch gunmen. Clint, in his role as a dignified businessman and excellent poker player using the name of Charles Martinez, purchased the two ranches with his gambling money. The two previous owners were glad to take the money and head back to Tennessee and family.

A pleasant thought passed through Clint's mind as he remembered the total domination he had achieved over the Starr Ranch and their crooked plan. However, not a hint of expression showed on Clint's face as the messenger, the gambler from Sacramento, finished his stories. He even thanked Clint for being such a good listener and for the free drinks. The thought that Clint had just wiped him out at the poker table must never have entered his thinking.

Clint had spent considerable effort to leave his past, cover his tracks and start looking for a new life. Any plan to return to help those two young ranch families could bring the late Charles

Martinez back to life. This could be dangerous, as there had been too many hints of Charles Martinez being linked to the young killer known as Clint Mason of Manatee County, New Mexico territory. A plan must be developed that would help his friends, but not bring the law and his past down on their heads. In fact, his own life would be worthless if his true identity was discovered. A return to Bay Town, California, was in his future unless a better plan could be developed to protect those young ranch owners.

Chapter 2

Clint broke camp at the edge of town. The sun was just starting to spread its golden rays across the beautiful Rocky Mountains. A chill was in the air and it gave his excellent mounts the urge to get on with the ride. He had three horses and two saddles, both with saddlebags heavy with gold coins. One horse was always kept fresh with no load. Clint's sharp mind always planned for the unexpected, or at least kept many options open in case of an emergency.

He was an educated man with legal experience under Judge Brown, successful survey work for the railroad and a broad education gained during his five years at the late Ms. Jamison's finishing school outside of San Francisco. In contrast, the appearance that Clint had nurtured to hide his true identity was that of a rough and tumble trail hand with above average poker playing skills.

His six-foot plus frame was in excellent shape and his olive skin color gave a hint of his ancestry. His mother, a Spanish aristocrat from New Orleans, had married a Texas rancher. The Mason family had moved west trying to keep its two sons out of the festering Civil War that had overflowed into Texas. The mother had tried hard to give both her boys a topnotch education, even at an early age. Her death left a big hole in the family, but the father had carried on as best he could. The older son, Brad, had buckled down and taken over the ranch business. Clint, the younger son, just became wild and reckless. His excellent mind was put to use beating everyone in his hometown at poker from the early age of 14. His second skill, much to the displeasure of his father, was his outstanding ease with firearms. At the age of 15, he was a better shot than everyone within riding distance. Despite being small-of-frame and wiry, he had been in fights with nearly everyone around the area that wanted one. He had been beaten many times, but he always came back. He had been so tough and mean that eventually everyone just tried to avoid him. These days, Clint amazed himself that he had changed into a smart, slow-to-anger, deliberate and dignified gentleman, even though he still loved to play poker and to work on improving his gun skills.

His mother had planted in him the seeds of an educated person when she had him reading the literary classics by age 12. Clint remembered that, after leaving home, he had been beaten and almost killed in San Francisco at the age of 16. It was the late Ms. Jamison that had discovered the book of Shakespeare in his saddlebags. That book so impressed the school teacher that she took a gamble on him. Five years later, under her guidance, he entered a new world as a 21-year-old, 6' 2" well-educated gentleman.

The gold rush in California and the building of the railroads had brought huge sums of money to San Francisco and the Pacific Coast. In this environment, Clint Mason made a fortune at the gambling tables and he had done all this under the assumed name of Charles Martinez.

Chapter 3

The sound of distant gunfire brought Clint back to the present. The sun was now directly overhead. The warm rays had burned the early morning chill off the air. He had not seen any riders, but fresh tracks had been visible in front of him all morning. His slow pace had kept the riders and their wagon well out in front of his position.

At the next rise in the road, he used his sailor's spyglass to scan the trail ahead. The best he could make out at this distance was gun smoke up on the cliffs on both sides of the roadway. Clint guessed that the wagon and its riders were being ambushed by at least four guns. The ambush was well planned. The canyon walls pinched down the roadway with steep walls on both sides. The bandits had excellent positions to shoot down on those trapped on the narrow road.

If Clint could get to the next major rise in the roadway, it would bring him within rifle range. He moved cautiously to the crest of the last hill overlooking the ambush. His elevation was about even with the gun smoke rings drifting out of the cliffs. The spyglass soon located three of the shooters.

He could also see a little of the ambush site. One saddle horse was down along with one of the four team horses that had been pulling the wagon. An occasional gunshot from under the wagon proved that someone down there was still alive.

There was no way of knowing what was right or wrong, but Clint's judgment was that anyone firing on a wagon and riders from cover was in the wrong. With that decision made, Clint leveled off four shots directly into the rocks where the gun smoke rings were rising. A sharp yell indicated either a hit or extreme fear. It was only seconds before four men and their mounts were scrambling further up the steep slopes of the canyon. Even at this distance, Clint could see that one of the riders was wounded and he had a good look at all four horses.

He then turned his spyglass on the wagon. The people below showed signs of preparing to move out. He could make out at least four people releasing the downed horse and hooking up the three remaining pull horses to the wagon. As he watched, the group seemed to be made up of two men, a woman and a slim teenage boy. Very soon, a wounded man was placed carefully into the wagon. The two men and the boy mounted the three saddle horses and the woman drove the wagon on down the trail. Even at this distance, Clint could tell those people were very nervous. They had been ambushed while traveling on the main road through the canyon. If that was not enough to unnerve them, a phantom rider had driven off the attackers from cover, but never showed himself.

Clint kept his distance, but decided to follow the wagon to ensure that they got to the next stop safely. The next town and trading post was about 50 miles. Clint had traveled this road several times over the past year. The town up ahead had a man that pulled teeth and treated any animals or people that needed medical attention. Clint doubted the man was a trained medical doctor, but he had plenty of experience setting broken bones, fixing gunshot wounds, pulling teeth and caring for horses. A small town in this rough western area was lucky to have such a man.

Chapter 4

As Clint rode down the main street a good two hours after the wagon, he searched the hitching rails for the four horses used by the ambushers. First, he saw the wagon from the trail ambush. It was being unloaded at one of the two general stores along this town's main street. The lady and a skinny young boy were talking to a man from the store. He had an apron on and was helping direct the unloading. No one paid any attention to a slow-moving, dusty cowboy and his two trail horses.

Excitement jumped into Clint's throat as he spotted at least two of the four horses he had seen ride away from the ambush. The first horse was easily spotted. It was a shiny black with white splashes on both front legs and one hind leg. The second horse was less noticeable, being a drab chestnut color. However, Clint's excellent sense of horse flesh ranked this chestnut bay as the best of the four horses he had seen in that canyon. The saddle and hardware on the two horses was worth a year's pay for most cowhands. The owners of those horses tied in front of the best hotel and saloon in the town were not ordinary cowboys. If anyone had been watching this drifting cowboy, they would never have suspected the close examination Clint had given the wagon and then the two horses.

He moved down the street slowly but without hesitation to an alley that led to an old livery stable.

The arrangements were made for his three horses, and he was given directions to a clean, cheap room and a good meal. The stableman suggested that he shop at the old general store where the wagon was being unloaded. The much bigger and newer general store was not to the liking of the stableman. A few questions and the stableman leveled about his suspicions of the trustworthiness of the bigger store owner, a Mr. Henry Johnson. He had moved into this town a year ago out of a Durango chain. He first undercut the prices of the original general store. Then, over the past six months, the freight loads coming to the older original general store were either robbed or bushwhacked between Durango and here. The freight load that had just come in was one of only a few that had made it through with its load complete. The driver had been shot, but should be okay after treatment to his flesh wound. The lady, Ms. Melanie Greene and her son were bringing a load of supplies from Durango where she had closed her store after the death of her husband. She and her husband had worked with the original general store manager, Rob Jones, here in town over the past several years. They had shared the cost of bringing supplies from St. Louis to Durango, then split the load for some to come on to this town, Cortez. The arrangement had worked well for both general stores until some months ago. Now, the loads from Durango were being robbed or delayed. Consequently, the freight companies were charging more to make the hazardous run. After the death of her husband, Rob Jones and Melanie Greene agreed to merge their two stores into one. She could bring her child to this smaller, but previously safer town.

11

The stableman was a lot of help with his open talk about the town and its people. It gave Clint a good feel for the situation and he felt sorry for the lady and the store owner of the original general store. The west had a lot of honest, hardworking people. However, without much law to protect them, those powerful enough took advantage of the weak and set their own rules. That little familiar burn was developing in Clint's chest, a burn to rebalance the odds in favor of the good folks. This do-gooder attitude, while familiar, was something of a complicating factor for Clint and for his own safety and identity.

His central purpose was to head to California to help save two ranches from this same type of lawless terror. This situation was a distraction he did not need, but the pull to set things right was very strong. His parents had implanted in him the seeds for justice to all people. Then, Ms. Jamison, his master teacher at the boarding school north of San Francisco, had refined his desire to treat all people fairly. His short apprenticeship under Judge Brown of San Francisco had provided Clint with more of the legal aspects in regard to justice.

Chapter 5

The back street hotel that the stableman had recommended was clean and simple. A brief cleanup and a short rest after the 50-mile ride into Cortez prepared Clint for a night's gambling and more research. The best place to start his mission was the big new hotel and saloon where the two suspects' horses were tied. Clint had already decided to make the big chestnut bay a part of his own string. That is the least payment those four ambushers would make. Clint knew himself to be ruthless and without mercy if the situation called for those actions. He also knew the risks involved with setting your own law and enforcement. His history had been to be judge, jury and executioner. These methods also brought the possibility that others would treat him the same way.

A satisfying late dinner of steak and potatoes in the fancy hotel dining room overlooking the gambling tables was a great start. Spotting his prey was not difficult. The dress and, in particular, the gun belts of three men at a back table of five caught Clint's attention. His ability to judge people was a skill that had served him well both in playing poker and in the art of survival in a lawless land. His patient observations finally paid off. It was almost two hours after Clint had first selected his targets that the real brains and power joined the table. This must be Henry Johnson, the owner of the big new general store that the stableman had described.

A well-dressed gentleman in his early forties held the attention of the five card players. Even at this distance, Clint could tell these men both respected and feared this man. The way he held himself and his confident moves were a caution for Clint. The only man at the gambling table with whom Mr. Johnson was carrying on a conversation was probably the rider of the chestnut bay.

Clint's move down to a gambling table near the six men was smooth and without notice. He waited for the right table and seat to become available, and then moved in with a casual attitude. His contribution to the pot was greatly appreciated by the other card players. He would have to listen and learn. The feeding of steady money into the hands of his fellow players lubricated the conversation. Clint's card skills were so superior to the other gamblers that he could distribute the winnings around the table at his will. His investment in the table was paying off with increasingly loose lips. The flow of liquor was probably an equally contributing factor. Clint kept a steady supply of chips in front of him so no one suspected he was feeding the table. He won just enough small pots to prove his skills, but passed on all the large table stacks.

The table of six players next to Clint finally broke up. Clint smoothly dismissed himself and slipped out the side door of the saloon. The six men were still at the hitching rail in front of the hotel. When Mr. Johnson turned into the hotel lobby, Clint's judgment was verified. The riders of the chestnut bay and the black horse with the white stockings were exactly as Clint had guessed. A subdued smile appeared as his judgments were proven correct.

Clint followed the two riders at a safe distance until they turned into a rambling type of bunkhouse at the edge of town. The complex had a large barn and corral with a dozen horses, a bunkhouse that could sleep at least 20 men and a nice home that faced away from the barn toward a well-kept for front yard. This no doubt was the operating base for this gang. Clint settled into an out of sight nook across the street from the complex and waited. It was after midnight when the well-dressed gentleman Mr. Henry Johnson – the apparent leader – rode into the front yard. A man came out of the house and walked the boss's horse around the house to the barn. Clint was impressed with the high style of living of this "gentleman" – who might also be described as master crook and gang leader.

Within a few hours of arriving in this town, Clint had learned a lot about his target mission. The next phase was to plan... and then act before heading on to California. The real challenge would be to leave the mother and son safer than they were before he got involved, while not losing his life or harming any innocent people. He had learned that the woman's name was Melanie Greene and her son was Jeff. Her late husband had been a respected businessman and citizen. The rumor was that she had been an equal partner in the general store with outstanding looks complementing her intelligence. Clint was determined to save her and her son from harm.

Chapter 6

A late morning breakfast at the café the stableman had recommended was a good beginning to the next day. The locals were still having coffee at a big round table at the back near the kitchen. So, he selected a small table near enough to eavesdrop without notice. Clint recognized the old general store owner even without his apron.

It didn't take long before the conversation got around to the attempted hijacking of his last freight load. Ms. Greene and her son, Jeff, were okay, but shaken. The wagon driver was recovering just fine. His entire freight load had gotten through without damage. This was the most expensive load he and his new female partner from Durango had attempted to make.

The store owner then went into details about the shootout and about a mystery gunman that was never seen. Ms. Greene thought that one of the horses that the robbers had been riding was in this town. She was not completely sure, but it sure looked to her like the black horse with white leg stockings one of Mr. Johnson's men often rode. That same man had been involved in two recent shootouts.

The table discussion gradually got very heated about Mr. Johnson, his crew and his operations of hotel, saloon and new general store. There was no love lost between this group of local businessmen and their new rich and brazen competitor. A lot of local problems had started soon after Mr. Johnson had moved into town. At first, everyone had been excited when he started investing in the town. He upgraded one of the hotels and a saloon to be the best in the area. The purchase of the best home in town and the building of a big new stable with a large bunkhouse had also been welcomed. The arrival of a half dozen men that spent freely on food and drinks was at first another pleasant addition to the town's commerce. Then, the opening of a completely new large general store that sold items considerably below cost set a negative tone. Mr. Johnson's men were often heard intimidating local men, and at least two gunfights had killed visitors at the saloon. They were officially judged self-defense based upon the testimony of Mr. Johnson's men and the bartender. The local sheriff was no match for those men, so he just stayed out of the way.

Clint now had enough information and gossip to set his goal. The next task was developing a plan that would not identify him nor bring harm down on the locals, especially Ms. Greene and her son. Another piece of the puzzle that Clint would like to uncover was the source or origin of Mr. Johnson's funding. Clint was a big believer in the method of detective work that followed the money. His experience had taught him that money or riches were at the core of most troubles between people. Pride and egos were close seconds. When you put money in the hands of an ego-driven man, the law, justice and fairness all took a back seat.

A couple of days hanging around town using the excuse of repairing his riding gear and resting his horse let him watch the big bay chestnut horse and rider. This rider was called Mr. Joe. It became apparent that Mr. Joe was the foreman or operating boss of the gang that was taking instructions from Mr. Johnson. Clint's trips in and out of the old general store buying travel items provided the opportunity to learn the date of the next expected supply wagon out of Durango. Just as he had guessed, two days before the scheduled arrival of that general store wagon from Durango, the chestnut bay, its rider and three additional men left the bunkhouse headed east. A mean-looking gun hand rode the black horse with white stockings.

The previous day, Clint had checked out the trail east to Durango to locate the most probably sites for the expected ambush. He had also located the six prior hijacking sites. This gang was very good at selecting sites that gave them the advantage of good escape routes if things went wrong. Clint prided himself in his own planning skills. The location chosen for his planned surprise was well ahead of the new freight wagon's arrival. In preparation, Clint had left two of his horses spaced out along the route the day before. For his plan to work, he had to ride his first mount hard to loop far around the gang so as not to alert them. Then he would tie up his tired horse and rely on the next fresh horse to take him back onto the trail and his selected bushwhack spot. His third horse was still a half-mile further east so he could leave a trail headed east, after the kill. This all assumed he could down all four gunmen without getting himself wounded or killed.

They key was to drop at least two of the

gunmen before they sought cover. He probably had no more than two hours before the freight wagon would reach this section of the trail. A drawn out gunfight could ruin his plan to remain hidden and unidentified. He also didn't want the chestnut bay to be injured. Clint did muse over his attitude that a prize horse was more important than the lives of bandits.

Clint had just gotten settled in his position when the four would-be bandits came around a bend just west of his hiding place. The four men were joking among themselves and traveling without any idea that they were about to be victims. The arrogance and confidence of the four only boosted Clint's determination to wipe them out. These four had ambushed the fine lady and her son only a week ago. If he hadn't come along, Ms. Greene could have been murdered without anyone knowing who had done it.

Chapter 7

The first two shots out of Clint's rifle dropped the first horse and man, plus the last rider. The third shot missed the two hard-riding bandits. A hail of slugs came Clint's way and both riders put their shots toward his position. Taking slow aim, Clint dropped the third man off the black horse as he headed up the steep slope away from the shooting. The chestnut bay and his rider had pulled up behind a big rock outcrop next to the trail. As soon as Clint had dropped the third gunman, a quick position change was made. The only bandit left apparently missed Clint's move because he was still sending a steady volley of lead into Clint's old hiding place. The gunman on the chestnut bay had pulled into a crevice between the vertical sheets of hard rock. The rock sheets were running at about a 45-degree angle away from Clint. A little calculation for ricochet bullets and Clint let his new position be known with a volley of shots into the void between the two sheets of rock. There may have been a grunt or groan from behind the rock shield, but Clint was not taking any chances. He moved along on his belly for at least a hundred feet before resting behind a large boulder. He lay still for more than an hour. There was no sound from the rock outcrop. Then Clint saw the chestnut bay walking slowly out of the protected slice of rocks away from the trail. It was just minutes after seeing that horse that the sound of the freight wagon came to his ears. The speed of the wagon told Clint they were not stopping for anything. The dust and the noise of the passing wagon had settled before Clint ventured out from his hiding place. He went back and retrieved his horse then collected the chestnut. Then, shielding himself between the two horses, he looked into the rock-protected passageway.

Mr. Joe, the owner of the chestnut bay and dressed in all of his fine riding clothes and fancy gun belt, lay in a pool of blood. The ricocheting bullets had cut the gunman to pieces just as if he were hit with a sawmill blade at high speed. After stripping Mr. Joe of all identifying clothing and hardware, the body was dropped into a rock grave.

The next hour was spent hiding all traces of the gun battle. The dead horse was stripped of saddle and reins, and then dragged off to one side for buzzard bait. The other three gunmen were treated the same way, stripped and bodies hidden. Clint then had a string of horses with saddles to hide. He rode on east and picked up the third mount that had been positioned in case of emergency. This group of horses laid out a good deep trail away, east of the shootout.

It was almost dark when Clint saw a small herd of wild horses. This was the perfect cover for the extra horses. One of his own horses was left with the gunmen's mounts as he transferred his field pack to the chestnut. After moving the released horses into the wild horse herd, Clint found a good resting spot high above the trial. An all-night watch over the trail assured Clint that no one was investigating the shootout, yet.

It was Clint's best guess that Henry Johnson would personally investigate the cause for the wagon load getting through successfully. The disappearance of Mr. Joe and his gang would definitely serve to double his curiosity.

Chapter 8

The morning sun had slowly warmed the rocks around Clint. The night chill was gone, but a slight breeze made his leather jacket feel good. His eyes were getting tired from the constant search of the trail with his spyglass. With the sun now directly overhead, sweat beads began forming along his hat band. Several times the sweat burned his eyes, but he kept at his vigil. His patience finally paid off. Mr. Henry Johnson, sitting astride a large white stallion with two riders spread out in front, came into view.

Clint had moved his location a short distance west of the ambush spot. He had a good vantage point from which to watch Johnson and riders when they came upon the ambush spot. At first Clint thought the three would ride right past the murder site, but Johnson, being the keen observer that Clint had predicted, stayed right on target. The two front riders returned to the site and started searching the ground. It did not take long for the two ground walkers to return to the still mounted Mr. Johnson. The "king" sat his white stallion with erect displeasure as the two reporters spread their hands, signaling that they could not find anything.

Even at this distance, Clint could tell that the boss was chewing out the two scouts for incompetence. This was the opportunity that Clint had been waiting for. The king was in full view of Clint's sights and the two underlings were on the ground out of the line of fire. A single shot toppled him.

At this point, Clint put his other plan into motion. He had loosely tied the black horse with the white legs down the trail. A shot into the rocks near the tethered horse caused him to bolt into the trail in clear view of the two men. A few more shots around the feet of Johnson's men put them into their saddles and running away from this ambush. After their dust trail cleared the next hill back west, Clint went down and gathered the white stallion. He loaded up Henry Johnson's body and gear. A short chase and the nice-looking black was also in his control. A few hours of work to strip and hide Johnson's body and release the white stallion and the black free of saddle and bridle completed the mission.

His next chore was to get back to Cortez and await the outcome. He would have to circle the town and come in from the west. The chestnut bay would have to be hidden somewhere west of town so he could collect it on his way to California.

Melanie Greene and Rob Jones would have to make it on their own. The odds had been adjusted to give them a fighting chance. The information that Clint had gathered on those two gave them an above-average chance of success.

He had killed men to give these people a better life. The rest was up to them. In fact, most people would say that Clint had murdered these men from ambush without giving them a fair shake. This was probably true, but in Clint's mind these robbers, thieves and killers brought their deaths onto themselves. Clint just happened to be the phantom rider that delivered justice.

Two days later and a little worse for wear, Clint was saddling up the chestnut bay. Henry Johnson's men had roughed him up a little along with several other men. Anyone that was a stranger in Cortez took some harassing. The Johnson gun hands were frustrated and without a leader. Clint took the rough-up like a coward and agreed to get out of town. This style of departure was good cover for him. A western man that would not stand up for himself would not receive any respect. No one in Cortez would ever suspect that this easy-going and timid stranger had singled-handedly saved Mel Greene and her son, plus wiped out Mr. Johnson and his control over Cortez.

The one rumor that really pleased Clint was the story that Johnson's men, Mr. Joe and crew, had turned on him. The two surviving gang members had reported seeing the black horse with white legs during the raid that killed Mr. Johnson. Finally, after a couple of days of blowing off steam, most of Johnson's crew headed back to Durango. The town of Cortez, along with Clint, breathed a big sigh of relief.

The saddles and hardware off Johnson's horses had been stripped of the decorative silver, fancy leatherwork and identifying marks. As Clint tightened the chinches on these fine saddles, he had to give the late Henry Johnson credit for excellent taste in guns, horses and riding gear. The extra handguns and rifles were the best of any that had made it out west.

The chestnut bay had been left in a mud-laden,

swampy area where it had rolled in the mud and clay. The animal looked the part of a rundown work horse. Not one person in a hundred would recognize this dirty work horse as the same clean, sharp-looking mount of the late Mr. Joe.

Clint felt good about the justice he had delivered. The big chestnut bay was eager and strong under Clint's control. The west-bound trip was finally underway. He had pulled out of Cortez about noon under the watchful eyes of several mean-looking Johnson gang leftovers. The few catcalls in his direction were annoying, but that type of treatment confirmed the story that he had been run out of town. Several hours of hard riding and the golden sun was setting over the distant mountains. A few more minutes and the glare would be out of his eyes. As he turned in the saddle to look at his fine horse string, the golden-washed mountains east toward Durango towered into the sky. This was a beautiful country if you could live long enough to enjoy it.

He headed west at a steady clip, using the main roadway. Getting a lot of distance between himself and the Cortez killings would ease his mind. This trail was well-traveled with numerous campsites. It was almost too dark to safely continue when Clint spotted a campfire up ahead. The fresh, deep wagon tracks that Clint recalled before dark probably belonged to the campfire people.

A call out to the camp produced a timid response for him to approach slowly. Clint moved his horses very slowly toward the circled wagons and large campfire. A good two hundred feet away, he dismounted and walked slowly toward the light. A big, burly man came out to meet him with shotgun pointed directly at Clint's midsection. When he got close enough for the light to hit Clint's face, the man lowered his scatter gun and put out his large, meaty hand in welcome. He had recognized Clint as one of the fellows that had been beaten up by some of the Johnson gunmen. The wagon train man explained that several of his people had also been harassed and roughed-up back in Cortez. The wagon train had planned to spend several days in Cortez to rest up before the next long haul. The Johnson gang was on such a tear that everyone had decided to continue west for a day or two then make a good camp. They had found this much-used campsite with a nearby spring a day earlier.

As he walked into the light of the campfire circle, two young men came over to Clint. These two with their bruises and black eyes looked a lot like Clint's own face. They welcomed the new refugee with a handshake, a cup of coffee and a plate of beans. One of the young men took Clint's string of horses and walked them over to a tether line which held two dozen other horses. The food was great for a hungry man. The company was pleasant and such a change from his last two days in Cortez.

The group around the campfire was glad to see a new face so they could all tell their tales again. The big man with the shotgun appeared to be the wagon train leader. He gave a history of their travels out of St. Louis. The story soon came to their problems in Cortez. At this point, the two young men with battered faces eagerly jumped into the storytelling with their tale of their encounter with the gunmen back in Cortez. The old man put in his difficulty of getting the young men to go out of Cortez. The hot tempers of the youth took some soothing before they agreed to let the beatings go and get out of town. The wagon train leader said he recognized the type of men they were up against. Clint could tell that the tuck-tail-and-run method the leader had imposed on these young men still did not sit well with them. Clint tried to back-up the old man with comments that it was wise to pick your own fights and not be prodded into action on another's terms. Clint confessed that it was not easy taking a roughing-up and doing nothing about it. He shared his humiliations with the two young men and hoped they would enjoy the chance to keep living. The lively discussion and storytelling went late into the night.

The wagon train people were slow to start the next morning. A big breakfast was served to everyone with Clint getting a hearty serving from two good-looking women. The wagon master invited Clint to ride along with them, knowing that his horses and guns would be very useful if trouble developed. The young men had spotted the new rifles and handguns that were being toted by Clint's fine horses. This wagon train had only a few repeating rifles. Most of these people had muzzle loaders that they had only used for squirrel hunting. A few of the men had been in the southern army as conscripts, but had used their own firearms. The trail guide the wagon master had hired in St. Louis had warned everyone about the risks of the trip. It was common knowledge that several wagon trains had been attacked by Ute Indians just west of their current location. This story was the main reason for the wagon master to ask Clint to ride with them for awhile. The firepower that Clint had in his four repeating rifles equaled the total among the rest of the wagon train. The string of horses was better than anything belonging to this group of farmers from Kentucky and Tennessee.

Clint accepted the invite to stay with the group until they were free of the Ute territory. It was not an easy decision because Clint wanted to get to his friend in California. However, a week of good food and careful travel would help his horses and himself. Some of the ladies in this wagon train were the best cooks he had come across. Clint had dealt with the Utes a few times. They were tough warriors and hard bargainers in a trade. There was a good possibility that Clint could buy clear passage for this wagon train. His saddlebags had the silver decorations off Mr. Johnson's and Mr. Joe's saddles. It was almost a fortune in silver and Clint needed to get it out of his hands. The last thing he needed was to be identified with the silver off the saddle of an important man. He had also kept the fine saddles and hardware from those two dead men. Almost anyone could match the silver pieces to the markings on the two excellent saddles and bridles.

Clint let the wagon master and trail guide in on his plan to contact the Ute tribe. But, he did not share what items would be used in the negations to achieve clear passage through Ute land. It took less than a day's ride west before a Ute hunting party was encountered. There was enough signing between everyone to set up a meeting with one of the tribal leaders. The guns that Clint had on open display kept the young Ute hunters at a safe distance. There did not seem to be a single firearm in possession of this small band.

The permanent village that Clint was led to held over a hundred people with shacks, some log houses and a few stone fireplaces. These were poor people living off the land, but they were skilled in survival on a harsh land. He was greeted in broken English by a young man who had the only rifle that Clint could see among the half-circle of men waiting for him to dismount. It soon became clear that while an elder man was the leader, the young man with the gun and English was a favorite son. It didn't take long before the Indian leader wanted to know why this white man was traveling through their land without an invitation. Clint's memory of this territory was of their intense boundary protection which would only be violated for trade. His wagon train was passing through on the open wagon trail and would not hunt any game while in their land. However, he was here to trade for salt and water bags of strong goat skin. His people were going far west across dry land and needed more bags to carry enough water. He was also aware that the Utes had found a salt area and the wagon train people were short of salt and pepper.

Clint could tell by the reaction he received that he had presented good reasons for the traders. The leader was eyeing his repeating rifle, but Clint immediately turned his attention to a bag of silver medallions. The Ute chief quickly recognized their value for future trades. Clint wanted to bargain hard so that the Indian leaders would feel they had reached a good deal. The silver that Clint turned over was worth a lot more than the salt, pepper and water bags he received. Clint's skill at reading faces told him the Ute leader was pleased with himself for completing such a good trade. This was further indicated when the leader handed Clint a doe-skin ladies garment as a gift for his woman. The dress was beaded with fine handwork and was as soft as wet clay. Clint was pleased with the results. Another gift that was unexpected had to do with the promise from the Ute leader that his men would let the other Ute bands know about their permission to pass safely through all of the lands. The trade deal was a win-win for both parties. The silver from a dead crook would buy much needed supplies for the Utes. The free passage through this hostile land probably saved some lives and it certainly prevented the theft of these farmers' horses. The guide had told the wagon train people about protecting their livestock. This agreement would go a long way toward getting their people through this Indian country. Clint knew there would still be some renegade bands looking for horses if the pickings were easy. It was his intent to make those uncontrolled bands aware of the risks they might face.

The next four days, Clint spent a lot of his time out in front of the wagons making the show of guns and fast horses. He only encountered two small bands of Indians that were looking for trouble. A few shots at long distance, aided with his spyglass, spooked both parties. They did not want anything to do with a rifle that could reach them before they could even identify the rider. One group tried a second time by splitting up to make a wide circle around Clint. A shot in front of each party close enough to spook their horse stopped their second try. As one further demonstration of his fire power, Clint dropped a mule deer out in front of the retreating Indian riders. This skill convinced these potential raiders to hastily vacate the path of the wagon train. This deer would make a good feast for this evening's cookout. Clint felt he was far enough out of Ute hunting area so that taking this deer did not violate his promise to the Ute leader.

A good campfire was going strong when the first wagon came into view. The site had good cover from the wind, a freshwater spring and plenty of firewood. The deer was dressed out and ready for the cooks. Most of the water bags were even full by the time the wagons had reached the campsite.

The wagon guide reported the sighting of several small bands of Indians, but none had come close to the wagons. Clint reported that he had been successful in negotiating safe passage through this Ute territory. However, he cautioned everyone that small bands of renegade Indians still roamed this area and would steal anything... especially horses and other livestock. He did not mention his recent methods of discouraging two of these roaming groups of young Indians.

Night guards were used to circle the campsite and all horses were securely tied close to the wagons. A peaceful night was welcomed by everyone. The meal of fresh meat helped to satisfy the weary travelers.

Within a week, the wagon train pulled into a small western village. The trading post was well-stocked and the town had a blacksmith. The wagon master informed Clint that the group wanted to spend a few days before continuing their journey. This was a good chance for Clint to separate from the wagon train and head on to California. His horses were well rested. One of the wagons had been hauling his pack and extra saddles for the past week. Several of the young men and boys had been taking turns riding Clint's extra horses. It was good conditioning for them and great pleasure for the young riders. Most of these boys had not even seen such great horses, let alone had the chance to ride them. Riding a well-spirited horse was such a break after so many hours riding in a wagon. There was some sadness on both sides as Clint headed west with his string of horses, saddlebags and full stomach. He would surely miss the good meals, plus a couple of the pretty young women that had shown a lot of interest in him. It was over a week of being catered to that would be missed on the lonely trail ahead. He had enjoyed the company of good people as well as watching the close relationship shared by these farming families.

Chapter 9

The next few days of hard riding made up for the past week of slow travel with the wagon train. All three horses were in excellent shape. Frequent transfer of rider and saddlebags kept all horses at top traveling speed. At this pace, Clint hoped to make Carson City by the fourth day after leaving the wagon train.

It would be at least three weeks before the wagon train could reach Carson City. It was the plan of the wagon train master to take his people north out of Carson City up toward Oregon. Two of the Tennessee families had relatives that had moved to Oregon two years earlier. It was their hope that enough land was available near the Tennessee families for all of this new group to settle. They had gotten two messages last year that had described what great country it was, plus an invite to join them in Oregon.

Clint had never traveled to Oregon, but had heard there was some great farming land west of the mountains toward the Pacific Ocean. East of the Rocky Mountain peaks was much dryer land. It was good grazing land in some areas, but the rainfall dropped out on the western slopes of the mountains. In contrast, the western slopes, all the way to the ocean, had great timber growths as well as excellent land for gardens, fruit trees and grazing. This vision put the thought in Clint's head that he should visit that land sometime in the future.

Carson City was a rough and tumble town with some of the biggest gambling casinos east of San Francisco. Clint had stopped here on his way out of California using a cover name of a Starr Ranch gunslinger. He had abandoned that identity and the Appaloosa horse that went with it. Clint wondered if that beautiful Appaloosa was still with one of the wild horse herds east of Carson City.

The new Clint would have to avoid any association with the Starr Ranch. If he was to carry out his mission to help the two families near Bay Town, it must be done secretly. However, Carson City had some of the best gambling in the whole country. The love of card playing and of testing his wits against a sharp adversary drew Clint to one of the saloons off the main street. The café served up a great steak and the waitresses were pretty and friendly. Life was good. Clint felt great and took strength in thinking that no one would ever expect him to come back from the dead.

The cards seemed to favor Clint without him even trying. He knew how good his poker skills could be, but these games were like taking candy from children. In fact, his winnings were piling up so much that it might draw attention to him. The movement from table to table would help. He also pocketed his winnings between tables so a mound of money did not build up in front of him. It was after midnight when Clint excused himself from a poker table after deliberately losing three hands in a row. A casual stop at the bar for a quick nightcap, then out the batwing doors into the cool night. The sky was so full of stars on this clear night that it almost took his breath away. Clint had stepped off the boardwalk of the saloon into a side alley to just take in the star-filled sky. The tingling of poker chips, the music from a piano and laughter flowed out of the saloon onto the boardwalk. It was one of those few moments in life when everything seemed to be in order.

The click of a gun being cocked brought Clint back to reality. Two or three slugs hit the wall directly behind him. Only his instant action kept him alive. Those slugs passed right through the space he had been occupying just a split second ago. By pure instinct, he crawled on his belly straight toward the shots. The boardwalk was about two feet above the alley. A quick move and Clint was under it. Boot sounds came down the steps off the boardwalk directly over Clint's head. Four boots with spurs were standing in front of Clint's eyes, not three feet way. A third man joined the two, saying he knew he had dropped the gambler. The three searched around the ground for the body, talking about how much money they had seen this gambler win. When the realization hit all three at once that their target must be still alive, somewhere in the dark, they froze in their tracks. Clint was looking directly at their knees. Three or four shots into those legs brought out the screams of pain. Clint crawled back along under the boardwalk to the hitching rail. He was acting like he lost something in the dirt when the hoard of people curiously filed out the saloon batwings. He joined the crowd as they looked around the corner into the alley. Three big, tough-looking men were rolling around on the ground screaming in pain. A couple of lanterns were brought to examine the gents. All three had serious gunshot wounds in their legs. Two of them had the more serious knee-shattering injuries. Clint heard a few comments rumble through the crowd that those three mean men deserved what they got. It was finally discussed that they probably shot each other over money they stole from some good citizen. There was no sympathy in this crowd for those three. A doctor finally came on the scene and the men were hauled off to a makeshift treatment room next door to the doctor's office. The crowd mostly turned back into the saloon to drink and make up tales about the alley shooting. Clint, without notice, moved on down the boardwalk to the hotel where he had taken a room. That was a close call. His enjoyment of playing poker had almost cost him his life. He thought his actions had been subtle enough to go unnoticed. He didn't often make such mistakes. He scolded himself as he fell off to sleeping in a nice clean feather bed. He enjoyed being on the trail, sleeping under the stars and sitting around an evening campfire. However, a bed with a feather mattress, clean sheets and no worry about rain or snakes was another way to live. The contrast may be what makes each so wonderful and rewarding. It is like eating a meal when you are really hungry; everything tastes so good. A month on the trail will make a feather bed feel like heaven.

Clint slept late the next morning to get the most for his money and build up his courage to head on west. He also had to test the streets to see if anyone connected him to the shootings last night. He spent some time cleaning his guns and himself. Gunpowder smoke would stay with you for days if you didn't scrub it off with soap and oil.

He sought out the café where a great steak had been served to him by a pretty waitress. She gave him a nice smile as he took a table near the back door. If things went wrong, he may need to escape rapidly. She brought his order of eggs and potatoes with a sweet smile. It didn't take much encouragement to get her talking about the shootout in the alley last night. Half a dozen men had been in this morning telling the story about three of the meanest men in Carson City shooting each other in the knees outside a saloon. Everyone was sure these three were arguing over money they had stolen from other citizens. They had a reputation of robbing gamblers after they left a game with big winnings. The local sheriff had never caught them, but most people had pinned a half dozen beatings and robbery on the three. There had been at least four unsolved murders of gamblers with big winning streaks.

Clint loved listening to the story almost as much as watching his pretty waitress tell the stories. The girl-watching was soon stopped when the waitress's boyfriend came into the café. Her interest in Clint was dropped like a hot rock, but he had enjoyed it while it lasted. It was time to move on. There was not a hint of suspicion directed at him. He had done the good citizens of Carson City a real service, but he didn't expect to receive any thanks.

He had one more task to wrap up before leaving town. The pockets full of chips that he had acquired last night needed to be traded for real money. The gambling tables of Carson City all used the same poker chips, so it was not too difficult to go from one casino to another and cash in a portion of his winnings at each place. The trick was keeping the cash-in amount small enough not to raise any interest in himself. It took a couple of hours to wander around town, staying at one casino first then another until all his poker chips had been converted to real coins. The $20s gold eagle was the choice of most traders and gamblers. This new catch was added to Clint's sizeable load of gold coins. He then slipped out of town without another incident or notice.

His time in Carson City was not completely wasted as far as information on the Starr Ranch operations. A rumor was on the back streets that the Starr Ranch, Phillips Freight Company and a Chinese group were moving opium. The information was very sketchy and scattered. The most common focal point was the small port city of Creston, some 20 miles north of Bay Town. The harbor was not as good as the one at Bay Town, but ships were known to be moving in and out.

It felt good to be on the trail with well-rested horses under him. He would miss the feather bed tonight, but the memory of the near bullet of last night made the wide open space seem safer. A shiver went through his bones when he thought about how close he had come to being killed last night. He had thought his card winning had been unnoticed and smooth, but he had almost been proven dead wrong. That experience would add some more humility into his personal pride in his card playing skills.

Sacramento was his next stop. His looks would have to be changed to get him into the opium dens and bathhouses in the town's slums. If he could keep his identity secret, then maybe he could find the link between the Starr Company and this rumored drug-dealing. If he could find the source of funding, that would be a good place to hurt the company.

Chapter 10

The ride west of Carson City was across rugged terrain with very little water or shade. The area between Sacramento, California, and Carson City, Nevada, was known for roving bandits trying to pick off easy money from those city dudes out of Sacramento that travel over to Carson City for the free lifestyle that city offered. Clint had put on his trail clothing, and it carried plenty of dirt to give the impression of a trail-hardened cowboy. Thieves did not like to attack a tough character. They were looking for the easy marks. In contrast, the excellent horses that Clint was riding and trailing could cause some attention. A top quality horse was worth a lot in this western region, but Clint was well-armed and forceful looking. Whatever the reasons, Clint rode without difficulty the next two days.

The nights were clear and cool, but the daytime riding was hot and dusty. His evening campfires were soothing to the mind and body. He was still trying to develop a plan to persuade the Starr Ranch and company to abandon any interest in his two Bay Town ranches. He had been so confident that his last confrontation with the Starr Ranch gunmen would deter them forever. He had killed their best gunfighters and caused the disappearance of their gang leader and top gunslinger. The new effort had to be made from cover, but still deliver a message that would be well understood by the Starr Ranch management. It had to make the point that any attack on the Bay Town ranches would bring sudden, expensive and deadly consequences.

The first order of business was to learn more about the present Starr Ranch personnel and the resources under their control. This would be risky because not more than a year ago, he had spent a lot of time around Sacramento, Bay Town and San Francisco as the distinguished Charles Martinez. His gambling skills were well proven in this whole region. His work with Judge Brown in San Francisco to solve some of the railroad and mining claim conflicts had been quite impressive to those in that social and professional circle. The horse breeding and the development of a good cattle herd on his two Bay Town ranches was also recognized by the other big ranchers in the region. The last thing that was in most people's memory was the deadly gun battle on the streets of Bay Town that took Charles Martinez's life. The fight left a half dozen Starr Ranch top gun hands dead in the street. In addition, two of Starr Ranch's best men, a foreman and a deadly gang leader, disappeared that same night without a trace.

Clint stopped shaving for a few days and stopped bathing. He didn't know how long he could live with this dirty, rough-looking trail bum. He was lowering himself over a pool of clear water for a drink when his reflection almost scared him; the smell was almost as bad. He remembered using this disguise once before. It sure did keep the people away. Most people just moved away a little and then ignored the tramp without further thought. The last touch, a hunched back posture, added another dozen or more years to his age.

The arrival in Sacramento was under cover of night. He had joined a group of at least 20 roughneck, dirty miners just a few miles outside of town. They were all headed to the Chinese bathhouses to get some treatment of their mining labor pains. Most of the men did not know each other very well, even though they had gotten laid off from the same mining site that was closing for a week or two. The men had plenty of money, but Clint knew it would soon be gone. He drifted along with the group without much interaction. A couple of the miners suggested that Clint smelled worse than they did. It was all in jest, and then everyone just ignored him. Several of these men had been here before, so they pointed out the directions to the Chinese bathhouses and drug dens. One miner pointed out his favorite bathhouse. His story was that pretty Chinese women hauled hot water to your tub and for a coin or two they would wash your clothes and give you a haircut and shave. This was enough of a story to lead the majority of this group directly to that one bathhouse. Clint went right along with the group; his curiosity was up to a high level.

The back alley leading to the recommended Chinese bathhouse was dark and dirty. Clint could feel the hairs on the back of his neck stand on end. This was an ideal setting for robbery and muggings. It was his understanding that if you left these bathhouses and drug dens with any money, it would be lifted before you cleared the network of dark alleys. The leader of this particular band of dirty miners, eager for fun, probably never left the bathhouse with any money and thus had never been attacked.

Clint had left his good horses, saddles and money in a safe place well before joining this motley crew. He had acquired a horse that looked like the devil. The poor saddle was not any better. He smiled to himself as he remembered the trading that yielded him this horse. About a half-day's ride out of Sacramento, he had stopped at a small ranch to inquire about boarding his horses for a week or so. The young couple had a nice clean place, but there were signs that money was in short supply. This young couple with three kids was glad to board his horses and stow his gear for a fee. Clint could tell they were more than satisfied with his suggested price. They also directed him down the road to a stockyard that had work horses for sale. At the corral of the stockyard, Clint looked over the available horses. As a group, they were a sorry lot, but just the appearance that he had in mind. After a little closer look, one of the horses stood out. It was the most beat up looking horse, but had all the build and temperament of a quality animal. As he watched the horse move around the fenced in pen with the others, Clint made his choice. The stockyard owner was trying to sell him on a couple of other worn-out horses that looked pretty good. They argued over the prices with Clint coming in way too low. Clint was acting as though he had only limited funds and needed something cheap. Rather exasperated, the owner finally offered Clint the beat up and scarred horse, if that was all the money he could afford. Clint agreed to take that horse if the stockyard owner would throw in an old saddle and bridle.

Clint's good eye for a quality horse did not fail him in his purchase. The horse had probably been tangled up in barbed wire fencing. The cuts and tears had done a lot of damage to his hide, but no major injury to muscles or joints. Some of the cuts were still infected, but Clint knew how to treat those problems. His only major concern was the mental condition of this well-constructed horse. A fearful experience for an animal and a person can have a lasting effect on their behavior. Maybe a few days or weeks of good treatment and the horse might respond and replace those bad memories with some good ones. Clint knew animals and had the touch to bring the best out of most horses. The short ride before he had joined the miners reassured Clint that this animal had not been hurt seriously, and only his outer hide had been scarred something terrible. He doubted the horse had much concern for its appearance as long as it felt strong, well cared for and was fed adequately.

Clint mingled with the group as they bargained for baths and pretty attendants. The bathhouse and drug den was not big enough to take everyone at once. Some of the men wandered on up the alley to the next establishment. This delay gave Clint a chance to fade into the night.

Clint's original plan had been to participate with the group. But after some more thought, he realized that his normal youthful appearance would be revealed by a good scrubbing in a soapy tub. The old, dirty, hunchbacked drifter would disappear in the warm soapy waters and a young warrior would miraculously appear.

Clint spent some time nearly every day conditioning his body. Exercise was a necessity if he was to keep himself in top condition and be ready to fight for survival at any moment. He spent an equal amount of effort to keep his shooting skills at a high level. His poker talents were always at their best because the love of the game moved him to play at every opportunity. That love of the game had almost cost him his life in Carson City.

Giving up on the approach to find some information on the dealings in opium from within the warm soapy tubs, he was left with the choice to observe from the outside. He moved around the network of dark alleys with great caution. Three different times during the night he was approached about coming into one of the bathhouses. When the inviting young Chinese ladies got a good whiff of him and a look into that dirty bearded face, they quickly retreated. That kind of reaction from a good looking young lady was not good for Clint's ego.

A few night hours of moving around this Chinatown did not give Clint any new information. His next choice was to watch this community during the daylight hours. If major money was changing hands, it would be in the business community. The rumor that Phillips Freight Company was involved would be his starting place. He had spotted the freight company stables last night.

A slow breakfast in a café with big windows just down the street from Phillips Freight seemed to be the right choice. The food was good and some of the freight wagon drivers frequented the café. It was during the third morning of coffee, eggs and bacon that his breakfast location paid off. The Chinese men from the miner's favorite bathhouse approached the Phillips Freight office.

They were carrying a neat, clean package and then carried a different color package coming out. Clint recognized the overseas wrapping that was common for packages from China. This confirmed a part of the rumor about Phillips Freight and drug smuggling.

If the drug rumor was proving accurate, maybe the second rumor about the port city of Creston as the drug transfer point would also be true. During his fourth breakfast at the café, as Clint was deciding when to ride to Creston, a new voice was heard. Clint had seen the Philips Freight drivers going in and out of the office and stables often enough to recognize them on sight. A new customer at the table with the drivers was better dressed and seemed to focus their attention. Clint could not make out the whole conversation, but he did hear that the well-dressed man was headed out to the Starr Ranch. This was the real break that Clint was looking for. His best guess had this business-looking man making the cash transfer from the sale of the opium to the Starr Ranch. If Clint really wanted to get their attention, the loss of a big cash payment should do the trick. The roads out to the Starr Ranch were well known by Clint from his previous work in that area. He had spied on the ranch several times in his earlier life. A remembered ambush spot was already chosen in Clint's mind. It was far enough away from the ranch complex to avoid alerting them, but had excellent coverage for protection, escape routes and concealment. He did not have time to retrieve his good weapons and horses. His scarred and tattered horse and older guns would have to do the job.

The ambush site was just as Clint's memory had pictured. The main trail passed through some heavy timber with giant boulders protruding up out of the earth. Some of the rocks were 20 and 30 feet in diameter and over 50 feet tall. The valley floor around them was deep in pine needles and very flat. It was like a mighty giant had pushed the huge rock pillers up out of the earth in the middle of an ancient forest. The western cedars and pines in this area could be four and five feet in diameter and hundreds of feet tall.

Clint settled into a niche with his horse nearby. If the cash carrier came with too many riders, he would just let them pass. Several hours passed before he heard the sound of approaching hoof beats. It sounded like two horses, maybe three. His horse raised its ears and head a little, recognizing the sound of other horses. A soft hand on the horse's nose settled her down. Clint then moved toward the coming horses to put some distance between him and his horse in case she made some sound.

Two riders came into view. It was the well-dressed gentleman from the breakfast table accompanied by a hired gunman or bodyguard. The two were overly confident of their safety, being this close to the Starr Ranch. A clean shot into the bodyguard broke the forest silence. The man with the money responded immediately with an all-out run for his life. He was on a fast horse and the large trees were preventing a second clear shot. Clint's patience held him in check until the rider cleared an opening some one hundred yards down the trail. Clint hated his next choice, but he dropped the horse. It was too risky trying to hit the smaller target on a fast moving horse. The big, wounded horse slammed into a tree on the edge of the trail.

Clint was on his horse and at the crash scene before the man could possibly recover. The man never had a chance. The wounded horse had stumbled head down into the giant western pine tree. The man's body had been smashed between the horse's body and the tree trunk.

It took some heavy pulling to separate the man's saddlebags from the tangled mess. The bags were full of golden eagles; drug business must pay very well. Clint, with his big knife, extracted the bullet from the horse. Then a trip back up the trail to retrieve the loose horse and guard's body. He loaded the heavy body on the horse and covered the blood stains on the ground. A quick sweep of the area covered his tracks and any sign of an ambush. He kept off the trail until he could get rid of the body and release the horse. The only evidence left for others to find was the accidental death of the Starr Ranch horse and rider. With the disappearance of the guard and the money, it could be assumed that after the collision of horse, man and tree, the guard took the money and left.

Chapter 11

Two days had passed since he had extracted the opium profits from the dead Starr Ranch carrier. He had retrieved his horses and gear from the young couple's ranch east of Sacramento. A small payment in gold coins had made the couple happy beyond words. It was more money than they could make in a year of steady labor.

Clint had then put hard riding between himself and Sacramento. Using all three of his horses, plus the new rough-looking mare, his two days on the trail put him within striking distance of Creston. He needed to find a campsite that he could operate out of with safety. A number of old mining claims were scattered along this mountain range. Clint remembered that a lot of this had been abandoned last year when he had passed through this area. Many of the get-rich thinking prospectors had tried their luck. First, they would build a small cabin or shed, plus corral for their animals, then dig some test holes. It did not take long for these greenhorn prospectors to realize just how much hard labor was involved in looking for gold and silver. Most of these men lasted through one winter, and would then abandon their claim when facing a second one.

It was midday during his third day out of Sacramento when he came upon the right abandoned mine shack. The layout was a single-room shack attached to a log pole corral, plus an outhouse. The mine was just a big hole in the side of the mountain. It didn't go back into the hillside more than 30 feet. The log shoring in the mine opening was poorly done and thus dangerous, though it wouldn't take much to correct the braces in the mine to make a well-protected safe storage area.

This shack was not more than ten miles from Creston, located up on the mountain slope overlooking the Pacific Ocean. The small Creston harbor was very visible. The spyglass could even bring in the symbols on the ships and their colorful flags. Clint spent the next couple of days cleaning the cabin, bracing the mine and repairing the corral. A small spring off to the side of the mine had been channeled to the mine opening to wash the gravel and rock. The ditch had been broken in three places. It only took a few hours to get the water flowing back across the front of the mine opening and down beside the corral and shack.

All this physical labor felt good to Clint. He had been in the saddle way too much the last two weeks. Even though he had worked hard and steady to get his campsite in shape, he had also maintained a constant surveillance on Creston and the harbor. He could see a couple of short sections of the main north-south road in and out of Creston. The freight traffic was not heavy, but it was steady. Heavy wagons brought logs to Creston from north and south. Although Clint knew there must be a sawmill down near the docks, he could not see one from his vantage point.

He was tempted to go on to his two ranches near Bay Town, but that would be risky. The last thing he needed at this point was to be recognized. The information and rumors about the Starr Ranch provided enough justification for Clint. If he could stop the harassment of the two Bay Town ranches without going near, it would be safer for everyone. Justice would have to be delivered by a phantom rider.

The ten days of watching had depleted his supplies. The risk of a trip into Creston would have to be taken. He had the dirty clothes, hump-back and scraggly beard identity well practiced. A string around his neck, tied down to his waist helped him to remember the hump-back posture. He had to loosen the string if riding a long distance or it became very uncomfortable. The old looking, scarred black mare went well with his outfit.

He rode slowly through the main street of Creston, all the way to the docks. As he had guessed, a large sawmill and lumber yard was located right next to the dock loading ramps. The town must have a population of a couple thousand people and visitors. A large, new general store was at the east end of Main Street up near where the north-south road passed Creston. A much older grain and feed store was down near the sawmill and docks. Clint needed some fresh grain for his horses, gun cleaning supplies and other personal items.

The older store was more to his tastes. The shelves were well stocked, neat and organized. The older gentleman that was the apparent owner was gracious and business like. The lady at the cash register appeared to be about 60 and was probably the owner's wife. It took less than an hour for his purchases to be gathered and put out on the loading dock. He had purchased some extra large canvas saddlebags to carry the supplies. He paid in gold coins with only a slightly raised eyebrow on the lady's face. She was very cute as she slipped a big bar of free soap into one of Clint's bags. There was not a word spoken or any sign that she had noticed his bad smell and dirty clothes.

While spending his time shopping around the aisles of the store, he did pick up some information about his ranches. The young soldiers and their families did come to this grain and feed store occasionally. Clint overheard one of the shoppers tell the store owner that the ranches east of Bay Town had lost some cattle to rustlers. The person passing the rumor to the store owner had seen the two young couples at the sawmill in Bay Town. The two ranches were trying to sell logs to make some money. A few weeks earlier they had prepared a small herd of 50 cows that were ready for market. The ranches must have been under someone's watch because just before their planned drive to Bay Town stockyard, the small herd was stolen. A ranch guard had been left to watch over the herd. He was slightly injured when the cattle were stampeded.

The storyteller also reported that some of the Starr Ranch men were hanging around the cafés and saloons in Bay Town. This was something fairly new. The big shootout last year had left several of the Starr Ranch's toughest men dead. Bay Town had enjoyed a very peaceful existence for over six months before some new Starr Ranch men started coming back. The troubles at the two ranches east of Bay Town also started about six or seven months ago. Bay Town had a sheriff, but he was no match for these new gun-carrying men from the Starr Ranch. The storyteller also heard that those 50 stolen cows were driven to Creston and sold to the biggest new general store here. The store owner did know that the new store was undercutting his prices to almost his cost. Starr Ranch men, if they came to Creston, would hang out up at the new general store. They never came down to his store for anything. Phillips Freight wagons that met the ships from China also stopped at the biggest new general store. Clint busied himself behind the store shelves until the tales were all told. He acted as if he had no interest in the problems of others.

This information was enough for Clint. He now felt justified to take whatever action that this situation called for. The first order of business was to recover the price of those 50 head of cattle. His next stop would be in the jaws of the lion. He would go into the other general store and size up the enemy. Coming face-to-face with these people would prove whether or not his disguise would fool them. The risk and challenges raised his heart rate. Hopefully his outward appearance remained cool and collected.

He hitched his beat-up, old-looking black horse to the rail directly in front of the new general store. His movement around inside the store went without any notice. A box of .44 shells was his only order. A small-framed clerk went into the back and brought forth his shells. While paying for the cartridges, he asked about buying a steer for his camp. The clerk led him through the back storage room and warehouse to the pens out back. That was just what Clint had hoped would happen. His eyes took inventory as he stumbled along behind the impatient clerk. Once in the back area behind the warehouse, Clint could see at least 40 head of his well-breed beef stock. The brands had been only roughly touched with a hot iron to confuse Clint's old ranch brand. Apparently, these rustlers were very confident of their safety. This also confirmed that the general store owner had to be in on this rustling scheme. Clint could see some of his cattle hides stacked next to the warehouse ready for shipment. That meant that they were slaughtering the animals right here and selling the meat and hides. A large three-year-old beef cow was pointed out to the clerk to get a sales price.

The walk back through the warehouse and back storage rooms gave Clint another chance to scan the place. It was well-stocked for such a small town that had a second general store. Clint would guess that this big new store owner planned to be the only general store in Creston very soon. Smiling inside, he waited for the price the store owner would place on the single steer. That unit would be the multiplayer for the 50 cattle that had been stolen from the two Bay Town ranches.

The store owner did some figuring behind the cash register, then came forth with a price of $4. Clint suggested a price of $2 per head, but the man held firm. It was then set in Clint's mind that this store owed his ranch partners $200. The next task was to extract that sum.

With a clumsy gesture, Clint pulled a hand full of golden eagles from his leather pouch and handed one to the store owner. Clint kept his head sort of tilted down counting his coins while he waited for the change. The hesitation on the owner's movement to the cash register was evidence that the man had taken a good look at Clint's money pouch. Just as Clint had expected, the man told him about a poker table down the street. The gaming tables were in the back room of the Blue Star Café. He also told Clint that the bar had the prettiest barmaids north of San Francisco. He thanked the man for the steer and the information on the poker tables. The trip up to his cabin would take a day or two, but he would be back for the weekend. His question about the hours of operation for the café and gaming tables brought the "never closed for business" response. The sly smile on the store owner's face told Clint that this man was sure he had found an easy mark. This idea in the man's mind would probably keep any bushwhacker off his golden eagle pouch until he returned.

Clint led the beef cow up into the woods a good distance before tying it up. The next two days of watching the big general store and café gave him a pretty good overview of the traffic. He did recognize the Starr Ranch brands on a half dozen horses. Each rider's face was burned into Clint's memory along with his mount. When he had a good feel for Creston and its visitors, he headed back up the mountain to his shack. He was also carrying information on the arrival of a Chinese ship.

A reloading of supplies, a checking of his guns and ammo and tending his horses and one cow and he was ready for some dangerous action at the café's backroom poker tables. He knew himself to be overly eager for some poker and its risk-taking. It was a real flaw in his character, along with being an assassin. He had some good qualities, but this was not the time to go over them. The tough-minded fast-shooter with sharp gambling skills was the current requirement. Over the past couple of years, he had prided himself in some new patience. But here he was walking into the lion's den, just because that store owner and Starr Ranch men had stolen livestock from his old ranch. There must be a better way, but his temper was pricked and he craved action and justice.

Chapter 12

It was late evening when Clint entered the café for a steak dinner. The store owner was right. The café and the bar in the back half were being served by four very pretty young ladies. The bartender was rough enough to cut wood with his bare hands. A mental note to Clint's brain: don't get drawn into a fist fight. The batwing doors between the café dining area and the back room saloon and gambling tables were bracketed by two tough-looking bouncers. This setup should have given Clint enough warning to just eat and run for his life, but his mind was made up, so more facts were not needed.

A glance between the bartender and the two bouncers told Clint that he had been expected. This was another reason to finish his meal, his second drink and slip out the door he had come in through. The challenge was clear and Clint could not make himself walk away.

To set the stage, Clint ordered two more double shots of whiskey. He was outwardly showing the signs of a little too much drink, while in fact, Clint had consumed very little. His sloppy appearance and poor table manners had allowed him to spill most of the drinks without anyone noticing. His plate was slid back as he steadied himself for the walk through the batwing doors and into the jaws of the enemy.

Big smiles emerged from two of the pretty barmaids as they folded Clint into their arms. They guided him to a back poker table. He fumbled around two of the chairs until he flopped into the one with his back to the wall. The table's dealer was unhappy, and so were two of the other players. It was a table of five players and the house dealer. This was a team sport evidenced by the slight looks Clint picked up between the dealer and two of the players. These two players were dirty cowboys with few card skills. They were just spending money and enjoying the service of two beautiful women. The ladies were well trained in their trade, offering the pat on the back, close moves to serve the drinks and more cleavage and leg than those boys had seen in years. The third man was a businessman by looks. He did not seem to know any of the other players, but had a serious and alert look about him. He did not fit into the setting very well, so Clint would have to withhold judgment. This businessman also had a good sized stack of chips in front of him. He either was winning or had brought a lot of money to the table.

The game was five card stud. That made for a fast game, but not for very big pots with each hand. The two cowboys were slow to bet but they were enjoying the game. The businessman showed very little expectation on his face. The dealer and the two poker players with tied down guns were not happy with the cowboys. Clint noticed an eye signal from the dealer to the two pretty barmaids. The drinks and service to the two cowboys became slower and slower, plus fewer smiles. This treatment paid off as the two cowboys excused themselves after a couple more hours. A slight smile turned up in the corners of the dealer's mouth. Only a very observant person such as Clint could have noticed it. The table was now to the liking of the dealer and his two gun-carrying partners.

The businessman had shown no reaction to the departing of the two cowboys. He had held his own since Clint had joined the table. The two cowboys had just about lost all their table stakes. The two gun hands and Clint had increased their chip piles. Soon after the departure of the cowboys, the pace at the table picked up. The betting got much heavier and Clint had to up his playing skills. The dealer was giving the two gun-toting card players some signals. They were very little signs but Clint decided to play into them. It took less than an hour of fast-paced play until Clint had cleared the two gunmen out of table chips. The businessman had lost just a few chips from his stack.

Clint was expecting some action from the two gunmen very soon. He had shifted his position in his chair several times. This movement had allowed the movement of his extra gun down to his lap without notice. The uproar came almost without warning. Clint had seen the flicker of eye contact between the dealer and the gunman directly across the table. The gunman thrust his head forward and turned over Clint's hole cards.

Clint's eyes were observing the card trick as if it was in slow-motion. The gunman had palmed two extra cards. His motion to move his hand over Clint's cards was a move to exchange Clint's hole cards. The second gunman was pulling his gun as the cards were being exchanged. The average person would be caught completely off-guard by the first action. They would never remember that the second gunman was drawing before the cheating cards were switched. Two bullets only split seconds apart ripped through the poker table. Both gunmen had guns drawn but had not come to bear on Clint. They were both screaming that the dirty scum was cheating. The two gunmen flew backwards as the impacts of Clint's .44 caliber shots hit dead center. Both gunmen's firearms discharged harmlessly into the floor. A sweep of Clint's hand across the table removed the cheating evidence that the first gunman had placed in front of Clint. The table action didn't take two seconds from start to finish. Clint's sleight of hand removing the cards was missed by everyone due to the gun explosions.

The dealer was saying that the trail bum was cheating. The businessman, recovering from his fallen position on the floor, reached over to Clint's hole cards and spread out all five of them. This revealed a hand of two pairs, jacks and nines. The other hands were then turned face-up. The man that had started the challenge of cheating had three queens. His hand was the winning hand on the table. The dealer could only look on with complete disbelief. If he was to push his charge of cheating, it would become clear that he knew the cards in Clint's hand.

The crowd around the shootout agreed that these two gunmen had tried to kill the dirty trail bum for beating them at poker. It soon became clear that these dead men had very few mourners in this building. The big bartender, from behind, grabbed Clint by the throat of his jacket ready to toss him out. The crowd reacted with furious shouts and the bartender let go of the death-hold he had on Clint. The powerful hands of that giant of a bartender had just about choked the life out of Clint. The choke-hold the bartender had put on Clint had just about crushed his windpipe. The bartender's hands were like a death grip. The man was almost double Clint's considerable build.

Coughing and choking, Clint got his chips cashed in with the help of several onlookers. He tucked his winnings into his jacket and stumbled out the front door to his sorry-looking horse. The big bartender and another gun-carrying man watched from the front porch as he rode into the night. Clint had in his jacket the full payment for those 50 head of cattle that the Starr Ranch had rustled. His head was still throbbing from having the blood circulation cut off to his brain. He wanted to laugh about what he had just done, but that fool play had almost cost him his life. Reducing risk, playing smart and being patient were skills needed to survive in this lawless land. He was very disappointed in himself for losing control purely for the pleasure of vengeance.

The killing of those two gun hands wouldn't end where they fell. Those two men were for sure connected to the general store owner and the Starr Ranch. The drug smuggling operation was also tied into the Creston docks, the general store and Starr Ranch. This operation was big and profitable. They would not allow a dirty, shabby, old trail bum to live after taking out two of their gun hands. Clint needed his best firepower rifle, spyglass and pure luck if he was going to get out of this mess. The worse part of all this was that he had created the situation.

Clint had left the hitching rail of the café at full speed. He had shown all the outward signs of tucking tail and running. This illusion was complete into the night. Then Client did what he was sure would be completely unexpected by those on the porch watching him escape. Once he was out of sight, he turned into the dark forest and made a wide circle back so he could keep a watch on the movements at the café and general store. It was no more than ten minutes before two riders took off at full gallop up the path Clint had taken. A few minutes later, the big bartender then walked up to the general store.

Clint was trying to decide if he should move from his hiding place when a buckboard came up from the shipping docks to the back door of the general store. The store owner, bartender and two other men carried several packages into the back storage room. These packages had the same sea travel wrappings that Clint had seen on the Sacramento bathhouse drugs. Just like in Sacramento, two clean packages were handed over to the buckboard driver and sidekick. Those packages would be gold coins if Clint's guess was right, a very tempting situation. He was already in big trouble for winning at the poker table. This decision would be no more risky than what he had just done. But it would pay a lot more and get at the heart of the Starr Ranch drug business.

He stayed on a back street, but one that was parallel to the movement of the buckboard. That load of money was headed back to a Chinese ship. This gang was used to doing this exchange without incident. The buckboard had only the driver and one guard. There were no mounted riders for security. The street from the main road past the general store and the café made three turns before it arrived at the shipping docks. Clint picked a blind spot between two bends so his action could not be seen either from the docks nor the café porch.

A quick switch was made of his horse with one at a side hitching rail. A discard of his hat and a big bandana tied around his head like a dockworker along with an upright stance made his transformation complete. He looked a good foot taller than the old trail bum. He lurched directly in front of the single-horse buckboard causing the horse to rear up and stop completely. The shiny rifle barrel was pointed directly at the two seated men. A harsh command was given to throw the money bags to the ground. The two men were so caught by surprise that they complied without hesitation. Clint moved his stolen mount to one side and slapped the pull horse on the rump. The buckboard shot down the street before the two men could react. A quick lift of the heavy bags and Clint returned to his own horse.

His old hat was quickly back on his head, the scarf tucked away and the two gold bags tied on behind his saddle. The dirty old trail bum and his beat-up and tattered-looking horse moved into the night.

He returned to his lookout spot to keep tabs on the general store and café. It was almost dawn when two tired riders returned to the general store. The store owner and several men stood around the two returning riders. It was plain from their body language that they had lost the trail of the old bum and his money. Clint took a wide berth around any sign of trail. He headed back up the mountain to his shack and a new plan.

The black mare was glad to get back with the other horses and enjoyed the extra grain Clint shoveled her way. Clint's other three horses had accepted the rough-looking mare without any difficulty. Two of the horses that had been pinned up in the corral were turned loose to graze in the open.

The count of gold coins he had extracted from the two separate ambushers was huge. This was more money than he had paid for the two ranches. One thought was the transfer of the money to the two ranch families. This would allow them to start over again somewhere else. They could just walk away from these problems. The Starr Ranch could just have the timber on those beautiful ranches. This was definitely a sensible plan and had minimum risk to his life and the ranch families. Justice and revenge were putting up a strong argument against this sensible option.

Clint spent the next couple of days mulling over his ideas while watching the town down below. He was in the mining shaft the third day when his place was invaded by four riders. The men looked over the horses in the corral then ransacked his shack. The mine was good protection but he was trapped. If they came up to the mine shaft, he could keep them out but there would be no way for him to escape. He had stocked the shaft with supplies for just this kind of emergency. There was plenty of food, water and ammo. Luck would have it that Clint had been rotating the horses between open grazing and penning them in the corral. This day the tattered black mare that these men could identify and his big chestnut bay were out grazing.

All his bags of gold coins were well hidden in the mine shaft.

The spyglass brought the face of each man clearly into Clint's memory. His hiding place back in the dark cave-like opening gave him complete coverage. The four men seemed satisfied that this shack was not the place for the dirty old trail bum they were searching to find. Clint's cabin was much too clean and neat for the trail bum they were looking to lynch. The four heavily armed men mounted and rode back down the mountain toward Creston.

The visit made one decision clear for Clint. The mining shack must be abandoned for another location. He remembered another old shed-like building on what used to be his ranch. It was a range building up on the far northern corner of one of the ranches. It was a good place for cowboys to overnight and store supplies. He would head down south to look from a distance at his old ranches. If the Starr Ranch cowboys were up to their old tricks, he might spoil another rustling job. He would ride a wide path around Bay Town. A day's ride and he was over the boundary of his most northern ranch. The shack was fairly easy to find with his good memory for landmarks. The building had survived the winter in great shape. Clint prided himself in the strong building he had redone almost two years ago. The ranch hands had probably not used the building since last summer. The two young ranch owners were no doubt keeping their men close to the main complex. That was another reason why the Starr Ranch could so easily pick off small herds of cattle.

There were no signs around the cabin that

anyone had used the building for over six months. The Starr Ranch rustlers apparently had not spotted this remote hideout. Clint cleared out the cabin a little and settled in for the night. He had brought the big chestnut bay and the tattered black mare. The little corral was still in good condition for his two horses.

He had been sleeping for a good six to seven hours when a distant sound came to his ears. At first he thought it was some animal out in the forest. A closer listen and the distant noise was recognized as the movement of several shod horses. The horseshoes would click on rocks or other hard surfaces. In minutes, Clint was dressed, horses saddled and moving into the big timber forest. He moved toward the sounds very cautiously. The morning daylight was just beginning to clear the mountaintops to the east. It was just light enough to make out the motion of half a dozen men on horses headed due south. They were in single file moving very slowly in this dim light.

Clint tied off his black mare that was carrying all his stuff. The chestnut bay was rested and ready for action. Clint led his mount slowly down the mountain until he hit the fresh trail of the passing men and horses. Keeping his distance he followed the sound of the horses ahead of him.

It was still twilight with a haze in the air when the horses up in front of Clint stopped. The sound of distant cattle could be heard as the wind shifted. Moving off the small trail and up along a line above the six men and their horses gave Clint the position advantage. It was hard to see the six riders but the soft sounds of movement below told Clint that the men were spreading out in a line.

The light was slowly improving so that an open area with 40-50 head of cattle could gradually be seen. The spyglass finally located two men down in the open field below. One was riding herd with the other sitting at a small campfire. These two night herders had no idea that death was waiting at the edge of the timbers.

Clint tied the chestnut bay and moved on foot closer to the six would-be rustlers. The light had improved so Clint could see all six men clearly. This also meant if they looked up the slope, they could see him. A big tree and some large rocks gave Clint the perfect spot from which to cause major harm with reasonable protection. He scanned the six men until he recognized the leader of the four, the one that had ransacked his cabin. Almost a half hour passed before the hand signal was given between the six men. They raised their rifles to bead-in on the two cowboys in the open field below. Clint dropped his man before any shot was fired. One of the five remaining rustlers yelled "Ambush!" and the five sped away back up the trail. The two cowboys down in the open field were immediately sending slugs toward the fast retreating would-be rustlers. Those two cowboys must be some of the ex-soldiers that Clint had left on those two ranches. Their quick response into action spoke well of their training and self-control.

Clint faded back into the forest and disappeared into the fog of the mountain's giant trees. Gathering up the black mare and his packs, this completed another task in his mission to save his ranches for those young ex-soldiers and their families.

Chapter 13

Le Chen was sitting in his well-finished office when one of his young Chinese helpers rushed into the room. The young man of about 16 was excited and rattling in Chinese. Le Chen held his hands up to slow the boy down. Then in a firm but friendly voice, he told the boy to speak slowly, but first take a big, deep breath.

The story slowly came out after frequent interruptions from Le Chen asking the boy to fill in some details. It appeared that a shootout had occurred last night at the poker tables in the back of the café. Two of the meanest men on the Starr Ranch payroll had just been killed by an old dirty stooped-shoulder drifter. The old man had beaten everyone at poker. The two Starr Ranch gun hands had drawn on the old man, but he had managed to kill them both. The bartender had also tried to kill the old man, but he failed in what the crowd said was a fair fight. The crowd had helped the old man cash in his chips and watched as he rode away into the night on an old rag-tag black horse. At least two of the Starr Ranch guards went into the night to hunt down the old man. Although the Chinese boy had not seen the actual shooting, the gossip around the café was that the old man must have the fastest draw of any man alive. He had shot both men directly in the heart after they had drawn first. The two Starr Ranch gunmen fired harmlessly into the floor as they fell.

The story continued: A little later that same evening, the buckboard that delivers the opium from the ship to the general store was robbed as it made the return run to the docks with the cash payment. Le Chen wanted to know more about the robbery of the drug money. Could it have been the same old man that had done the robbery? The Chinese boy was relaying the story that the driver and guard had brought back to the café. They had said that the man holding up the delivery of money to the ship was taller than the old man, much better built and was riding a different horse. He also looked like one of the ship hands with a scarf around his head and no cowboy hat. It was definitely two different men. The old man had been riding a very rough-looking black horse while the robber was riding a well-groomed brown with a white splash on its forehead. Besides, the old man had taken off in a dead run up the street toward the main road. He was last seen running for his life after the bartender had almost choked him to death.

Le Chen wanted to know when had this all happened? The incident was almost two hours ago. The bartender was not letting anyone leave the café until the guards had checked each and all. After the driver and guard returned to the café with the report of the robbery, things really got to sounding mean in the backroom of the café.

The bartender and one of the Starr Ranch guards from the general store roughed-up the buckboard driver and guard. There was no way a single gunman could have taken those sacks of gold coins without some shots being fired. It looked like his men had given up the money without a fight. If they had gotten off at least one shot, the other Starr Ranch men would have heard and then could have come to their rescue. Without any marks or wounds on either man, the bartender was having trouble accepting their story. At this point the café was cleared out. The Chinese boy did not know what happened to the buckboard driver and guard. As soon as the bartender let him go, he had come directly to Le Chen. Chen's two Chinese ladies that also worked at the café might give more details.

There could be some real trouble from the Starr Ranch men if that money wasn't found. Chen had already heard that one of the top hands from the Starr Ranch up near Sacramento had died and a huge amount of gold was missing. Now this second robbery of gold cash right here in Creston would cause the Starr Ranch men to be both alert and angry. Le Chen would tell all his people to stay clear and be very passive, to yield to any harassment that comes their way. Some roughing up would be better than death. Chen's men were good with knives and fist fighting, but no match for the firepower the Starr Ranch men carried.

It was mid-morning the next day when Le Chen got his first visit from the Starr Ranch crew. Four heavily armed men came into Chen's place of business. They wanted to look around for a tall man with a bandana and two large sacks of gold coins. Chen was completely cooperative and permissive even though anger boiled deep in his chest. The Starr men rambled through his entire building containing a dozen rooms and over 20 people. They spilled things on the floor, turned furniture over and roughly handled each person. Some of Chen's young ladies were terrified, but the hour of harassment was endured without any resistance from Chen's people. He was proud of how they controlled their feelings. The Starr men finally left in a huff when nothing could be found.

Le Chen calmed everyone down and they got to work cleaning up and putting his building back into shape. It took less than an hour and there were no signs left of the turmoil that had passed through his building and people. The few broken items were removed to the back repair shop. These items would be made whole again with only a few exceptions. A sigh of relief went through his building when the job was done and all were okay. Chen knew that this one visit may not be the last before the Starr Ranch people worked off their anger. He praised his staff and offered a short work day. This definitely seemed to improve spirits.

Le Chen's mind was in high gear working through these incidents in Creston. It appears that an old stooped-shoulder drifter had outplayed two of the Starr Ranch gunmen at poker. Chen knew the card dealer and the big brute of a bartender were participating partners with the Starr Ranch. It seemed almost impossible to beat the poker table with those types of odds and handicaps, on top of winning at poker, then survive a setup that had killed three or four men over the last six months. To outdraw two well-experienced gunmen from a seated position was a surprise, or even a miracle.

These thoughts triggered Le Chen's memory about a gentleman his great uncle in San Francisco had told him about. The man had saved a dozen Chinese workers during a gunfight between some claim jumpers and the railroad. The Chinese workers had been provided by his great uncle, Hoe Wang, in a contract arrangement with the railroad. Le Chen's own move to America had been arranged by his family and his father's uncle, Hoe Wang. In fact, this relative had set him up in this Creston business some ten years ago. Chen had long since paid the great uncle off and had seen his own business grow. He could now send a nice sum of money back to his family in China every six months or so. He and his two brothers that had come to America at the same time presently ran a network of trade between San Francisco and Sacramento. For years, Chen's family had not fully approved of Hoe Wang's trading business which included drugs, silk and young people. The trading in young females out of China was a lucrative business. These young women were sold as servants, low cost laborers and prostitutes.

China was going through a severe famine, opium wars and widespread corruption. One of the effects of these circumstances was that the infant death rate of female babies was triple that of males. These destitute families with young daughters could sell them to the people traders almost as a cash crop. Le Chen had seen this first hand in his own community. His father angrily disagreed with the practice. Le Chen was raised to respect all people and his family educated males and females alike. His father and grandfather had established and developed a thriving business of trade with the English. All of Chen's family was raised to speak, read and write the English language. That skill had paid off very well for the whole family clan until about the 1820s. By then, the drug wars and government corruption had become so widespread that the lawful business practices of the Chen family were put under tremendous stress. The Chen business had tried to advise and help hundreds of families to survive those hard times until it had all but bankrupted the Chens.

Word was spreading through the China coastal areas, especially reaching out from Hong Kong, that America was a rich country. Although the Emperor of China forbade the emigration of Chinese, many had left for work in America. Chen's great uncle Hoe Wang had escaped China as a young man some 40 years ago. He had set himself up as a link between people and businesses in America that wanted cheap labor and the unethical traders in China. Hoe Wang had made a fortune in coordinating this trade which included opium drugs and other commodities such as silk. Wang respected the Chen family's fair practices and ethical behaviors and offered to relocate any of the kinfolk that wanted to travel to America. It may have been a token gesture or maybe a bit of atonement on Hoe Wang's part.

The Chen family was known in their ancestral village in China as highly trustworthy and well-educated merchants. Le Chen's father served on many committees in their homeland. The Wang side of this large clan was much more rough-cut but had become very profitable. The Wangs were somewhat more aggressive in their employment and trade practices. The Wang family had used the Chen family as their business accountants for several generations. In fact, the first job that

Hoe Wang gave Le Chen when he arrived in San Francisco was the upgrading of Wang's business accounts.

Le Chen was no more than 16 years old, but well-educated... and he was an experienced merchant even at such a young age. He wore the customary queues (pig tails) as a sign of loyalty and allegiance to the Emperor, in order to return to China. The Confucian teachings were well set in the Chen family. Both the Chen and Wang families were primarily from the Kwangtung district of southern China. This area has also been called the Taishan region. The whole of southern China had been hit with death, famine, floods, British-China Opium wars and corruption. The autocratic rule of the Qing Dynasty was being broken up by gangs and rebellion. Poverty and starvation was widespread in China. Even with the threat of death from the Emperor for anyone trying to leave China, emigration was slowly building. Most of the Chinese that came to America during this tremendous upheaval had all the intention of returning to China. They came to obtain wealth only to send it back to their families. The name they gave to America and California was "Gold Mountain."

Chapter 14

California, or if you wanted to call it Gold Mountain as Le Chen's family did in China, had treated him well. He had arrived in San Francisco without a cent to his name, and his debt for his passage from China was owed to his great uncle Hoe Wang. His arrival had preceded the big gold strikes of 1849 and 1850 when California became a state in the United States. The time of his arrival, although purely chance, was a lucky thing. When California became a state, all free men that resided there also became citizens of the United States of America. This had proven to be a key ingredient in his development of his wealth. Hoe Wang had been a tough taskmaster, but when Le Chen's debt was paid, he was allowed to start out on his own. His excellent command of English, plus his trading contacts with his family in China, proved to be an opportunity.

With a small down payment, Chen took a lease on a China trade goods store near the San Francisco docks. While working for Hoe Wang, Chen had seen the huge markups that Wang put on imports from Asia. The demand was strong for any authentic merchandise from Asia. Ivory carvings, furniture and home decorations were being purchased as rapidly as they were put on display. The European and northeastern American businesses setting up offices and homes in and around the San Francisco Bay were decorating their places with lavish Asian flair.

Le Chen remembered with a smile how quickly his fortune had grown. His family in China had benefited greatly, as did thousands of hungry and destitute Chinese families that converted their furniture and home decorations into cash and food for survival. He was able to mark up his items seven, eight, and nine times their cost and still not satisfy the demand. He was able to bypass most of the graft and corruption in China by using the family. His constant dealing with a couple of the British and Chinese ships and their shipping companies developed good and fair working arrangements for all. These working arrangements with the shipping companies opened up his operation into both Bay Town and Creston. The docks in San Francisco were being troubled by dock gangs and government corruption. The two seaports in Bay Town and Creston, although smaller, offered excellent protected coves with deep-water ports. Le Chen set up a freight company to move materials from San Francisco to Sacramento with Bay Town being just about in the middle.

As far as finding good honest people to run his business, his family in China became the source. The horror of famine and civil wars continued to tear China to pieces. Families were desperate and willing to send their young people into bondage just to get them out of China. Chen's family would screen the young people and send only the best-educated and most honest. If any of the selected youths could not speak English, Chen's family ran them through months of English training before they could join Le Chen's organization in America.

This was like human trafficking but everyone was reaping benefits. It was considered illegal in California and a crime punishable by death in China.

Le Chen was importing about equal numbers of men and women. In contrast, the migration from China to California had been almost totally young males. Most of the young men were not coming to California to settle, but just to make money for their families back in China. The vast majority hoped to get rich and return to China as heroes to their families and communities. Most other immigrants to America came from parts of Europe, to escape their homeland with no plans of ever returning.

The young women and girls, for whom Le Chen was arranging transport, were from good families. In contrast, the young Chinese women that had been in many of the previous waves of immigration had mostly been put into prostitution or domestic slavery. Chen was determined to protect these young women and give them a chance for a fair and good life in America.

He set his immigrant women up in his own stores, cafés and other shops directly under his company's protection. Since his Chinese family had done excellent screening and had sent the best and brightest, he was able in return to send their families a nice sum of money for their services. These beautiful young Chinese women became a trademark of Le Chen's stores. His most profitable business was still his San Francisco Oriental Furnishings store which was organized with beautiful Chinese sales ladies making good commissions.

A steady supply of men and young beautiful women was needed just to replace the ones that were getting married. Thousands of young Chinese men that had come to California, and most of them worked to marry a nice Chinese girl. Le Chen had the corner on that market. Chen would split the dowry between himself and the young ladies' families. It was a win-win for all concerned. The family back in China was helped and happy; the two young people were happy and Le Chen got richer.

In addition, the trade of ivory carvings, silk items, Oriental furniture and Asian paintings was making Le Chen a truly rich man. He had been in America only 15 years, but was probably the richest man in Creston, California, though there were few outward signs of his wealth. The Starr Ranch men that had ransacked his office and shops had no appreciation for the value of those oriental items they tossed about so carelessly.

Along with his accumulation of a sizeable fortune, Le Chen had helped hundreds of families in his homeland. His smooth, meek manners and small frame completely disguised the shrewd businessman under the surface. His big heart was clear to those that had migrated to California out of utter poverty and chaos. His accumulated wealth and businesses enhanced his capability to aid even more people.

However, the expansion of his business at a hectic rate had not interfered with his personal development. Within the next month or two, he was expecting the arrival of a particular young lady. His family in Kwangtung had arranged for a marriage. She was a well-educated young woman from what was previously one of the best families in the region. The Civil War and famine had all but wiped out the Quinn family. They were eager to bond their family to the Chen family through this marriage. They also had reason to fear for their daughter's safety. She was a striking beauty with superb personality and nature. Kidnapping of such young girls was rampant throughout the region. They were then sold off for prostitution in foreign lands. The Chen family had helped the Quinn family numerous times to convert family possessions into food and cash for survival. The Quinn leader remembered the young Le Chen when he was doing trade for his father at the age of 14. The two family leaders agreed that it would be a good match for both young people and for their families. The proposition was presented to both for their thoughts. Wan Quinn was only 18 years old but very mature. She quickly agreed to the match. Her prospects in China were dim. Le Chen was now 30-two and very busy managing and building a rapidly growing business. The timing was just right for Le Chen. He had been thinking a lot about finding a wife and starting his family. The steady flow of beautiful Chinese girls and young women going through his business may have played a large part in his thinking. He knew the Quinn family and trusted his family's judgment.

The next task was to arrange the travel of a refined, beautiful Chinese maiden without risk of harm. Le Chen's contacts with the shipping company could help with the ocean travel. However, getting her from her village to the safety of the ship was a horrendous trip. The ship was scheduled to depart a Hong Kong port with some silk, ivory carvings and paintings destined for Le Chen's warehouse in San Francisco. The Quinn family had added a large shipment of oriental furniture. To accompany that shipment were five handpicked Quinn relatives, including one of Wan Quinn's brothers. Wan would be disguised as a boy laborer in shabby clothes and dirty face. The shipping order would specify that the Quinn people were to stay with the shipment until it was signed for at the San Francisco docks by a Le Chen Company representative. The instructions would also specify that the Quinn crew was to accompany a return shipment from the Le Chen Company back to Hong Kong. These papers would help with the clearance of the Quinn people through customs in China. Although trade with the Americas was encouraged by the cash-strapped Chinese government, it was still illegal for Chinese people to leave China. On the American side of the water, the policy on Chinese immigration had changed several times. Sometimes the Chinese were wanted for the labor to build California. At other times local groups would try to pass ordinances that prohibited Chinese emigration. San Francisco had stayed open for their arrival most of the time. However, several towns along the Pacific Coast line all the way up to Seattle had tried to return the Chinese workers to China.

Le Chen had put a lot of effort into keeping the communities near him welcoming to him and his various businesses. He provided high quality and inexpensive service, Chinese food cafés, home decoration goods, tailor shops, haircuts, baths and pretty ladies to wait on tables and be clerks. He did not provide women for sexual favors. If any business harmed or mistreated any of his girls they were cut off from the supply of the prettiest Chinese women on the West Coast. His reputation for fair and honest trading was widely known and respected.

Chinese men on the west coast also knew that if they wanted to marry one of the Chen ladies they had to follow certain rules. The biggest hurdle was getting permission from the two families in China. Communication with remote villages in China was difficult and took lots of time. The men also had to prove they could financially support a wife and family. A third procedure that related to their financial status was the payment of a dowry to the Chen Company, a dowry that would be split with the young lady's family back home. Then they also had to pass an interview that the subject young lady could witness in secret. In spite of all these hurdles, Le Chen was surprised that his supply of young eligible females could not keep up with the demand. He was even getting some push from his family in China to receive more young women.

The roving gangs and the Civil War had made life very dangerous for young women. Gradually, word came back to the villages about how their daughters and sons were making stable lives for themselves in California. The Chen family was recognized as a sponsor and a path to assist the miseries now facing many Chinese families. This reputation was, however, creating considerable risk for the Chen family.

Le Chen's father wrote on numerous occasions that their work was saving many people in China from starvation and saving the lives and reputations of many young women. Since it was still illegal to leave China, this work remained risky. But the Chen family had all agreed it was the price they were willing to pay. Le Chen's father, grandfather and great-grandfather had been civic leaders in their community as far back as anyone could remember. They were holding onto that reputation and the joy of public service as long as life permitted. The Chen family had lived in the same town for over a thousand years. Le Chen felt good in his heart that his efforts had helped his family to survive.

At a regular business meeting that Le Chen called every three or four months, he inquired about the Starr Ranch gold robberies. The Sacramento representative told the story about the Starr Ranch carrier running into a tree and being killed. The guard that was riding with the courier was never seen again and the total gold shipment disappeared. This guard was one of two men that had also beaten and raped one of Le Chen's girls.

Le Chen relayed the story of the poker game and shootout that killed two of the Starr Ranch's meanest gunmen in Creston. Only minutes after that shootout with a greasy old hunchback trail bum, the shipment of gold coins headed to the docks was robbed without a shot being fired. The driver and guard had not been seen again after they reported back to the bartender and general store owner. One of Chen's barmaids had been asked to give the guard a detailed description of the trail bum and his card playing skills.

A café operator from Bay Town then spoke up. He had this weird feeling that a similar thing had happened in Bay Town almost two years ago. The café operator called the story the "Bronze Warrior" tale. He described it as more myth than fact, but still many Chinese workers thought the late Charles Martinez was the bronze warrior. By many accounts, that man had saved hundreds of Chinese workers from being killed in the crossfire between railroad security, government troops and the looters of gold from some railroad tunnel excavations. This gentleman had an olive complexion and was thus called the bronze warrior. His gambling skills were as much of a legend as his mastery of firearms. He had been reported killed on the streets of Bay Town, only after taking a half a dozen men to the grave with him. That street fight had left Bay Town peaceful for almost a year. Only recently had the Starr Ranch gunmen returned to their old tricks and trouble-making ways. The Bay Town Chinese café owner continued the myth with the story that numerous Chinese workers had reported seeing the bronze warrior in places like Sacramento, Carson City and as far east as St. Louis and Santa Fe, New Mexico Territory. What continued to give this myth some life was that the two Chinese workers that had helped to bury the late Charles Martinez had secretly told friends that the body that was called Charles Martinez was as white as a ghost. The local sheriff and the U.S. Marshal, plus the judge in San Francisco, declared that Charles Martinez had been killed on the streets of Bay Town. No Chinese worker would dare to publicly dispute the law's findings. The myth continues to this day with Chinese workers in Sacramento bathhouses and cafés whispering that the bronze warrior was still protecting them. The recent death of the Starr Ranch chief courier out of Sacramento, followed by the mysterious disappearance of a huge shipment of gold, were seen as more proof.

The rest of the meeting went on as usual refining the coordination of the various elements of the business. The quality control reports were good. The slow-moving or non-saleable inventory was small and not growing. Le Chen praised the group for a job well done. He gave the shops permission to sell the slow-moving merchandise below cost. The new shipments were arriving with better quality and closer to the needs of their customers. The shops would need to make room for the new inventory. Le Chen would send out the new pricelist showing the reduced cost to his stores. The bookkeeping was kept central but each store was encouraged to keep their own accounts. These quarterly meetings gave the store managers a chance to reconcile their accounts with the master account. This was also the time when individuals could make their transfer payment amounts for the families in China, and exchange letters with families back home. Most of the letters contained thanks and blessings for saving their parents, brothers, sisters and grandkids. Often they were requests for some to return to China if the family head had died or had been kidnapped.

Le Chen left the meeting with the idea that the bronze warrior may be alive. He needed that man's skills to help retrieve his wife-to-be from a ship at the San Francisco docks when it arrived. His men were good fighters but not when compared to the use of repeating rifles and handguns now common in California. The myth was that this bronze warrior was fair and kind to the poor and honest, but merciless to the evil-doers. The many stories that were circulating among his people included the use of disguises to hide his true identity. The skills demonstrated by the old hunchback bum sounded very similar to those told of the bronze warrior. While the reported appearances of the two were worlds apart, Le Chen decided on a plan to investigate further.

Word went out to all his stores, bathhouses, barber shops, cafés and teamsters to invite the old-looking trail bum to visit him. If he was located and the invite was not successful, then Le Chen would travel to this man for a talk. It was three weeks before the message came to Le Chen that the old hunchback card-playing bum had been seen at a poker table. The old trading post and gambling room was located a half of a mile north of Creston City. It had originally served as a trade station for the local Indian villages and fur traders. Le Chen operated a small café and warehouse with stables there. The old man's wagons often overnighted and he would trade horses at the Chen warehouse corral. One of the Chen's barmaids at the trading post had told the Chinese café operator that the old man they were looking for was playing some friendly poker in the back room of the trading post. This man must be staying somewhere close because he had been in and out of the trading post several times over the last three days.

The café operator decided not to contact the gambler directly but sent a message to Le Chen. A dozen Chinese workers were sent out from the café to cover all trails leading away from the trading post. Each man was given specific instructions to stay clear and not be seen. Their only tasks were to see what direction the man of interest traveled.

They were not to trail him, only report back their findings.

Le Chen arrived the very next day after getting news of the reported sighting. He hung around the Chinese café because the operator said the old man had come there to eat the last two days. Chen knew his cafés served the best food in the region and at the best price. The wait was not long. The hunchback man arrived for a late evening meal in preparation for a night's poker games. A corner table out of the way of the door and with his back to the wall was his choice. This was exactly what Chen had expected. According to Le Chen's experienced judgment of people, this was no old crippled trail bum.

Le Chen bided his time until his man of interest had finished his steak. Then an after-dinner drink was offered to the man as an introduction for talks. By his body language, Chen could tell the man was at full alert. The story of the card table shootout in Creston came to his mind. The hand in the man's lap probably had already palmed a gun. Using a hand gesture, Le Chen requested permission to join the man's table. Their eyes met in a firm solid lock. The man then spread his hand out with palm up to accept the request. The other hand stayed under the table.

Le Chen had made up his mind that this old-looking man was most likely the bronze warrior of Chinese legend. A brief introduction from Chen that included the facts that he owned this café and several other businesses from San Francisco to Sacramento was given without asking any questions in return. A fresh cup of coffee was brought while Chen continued to give some personal background.

Their eyes made frequent contact as a softer look gradually spread across the old man's face. He slowly sat up a little straighter as Chen continued in his soft but excellent English. Without a single direct question as to the man's identity, Le Chen asked for his help. The first words from the old-looking man were, "How can I be of assistance?"

That response led into the long story of his expected bride. Chen's men were brave and they were good fighters, but no match for the many gunslingers between the San Francisco docks and his home in Creston. The payment could be whatever this man thought was a fair price. The risks could be very high. The threat of death would be all around such a rescue and delivery. Chen offered some gold mine claims with cabins that he had accumulated over the past couple of years. The offer of a claim with cabin and corral up the mountain that overlooked the Creston harbor and some of Creston's main streets brought the two men eye-to-eye with a big smile on both faces. This finally broke the ice and they adjourned to a back room for more detailed discussions.

Clint forgot about his plan for a fun poker game. Chen was in a position to help him break the Starr Ranch's obsession over his two ranches. At least his network of people would know much more about the local operations of this group than he had been able to uncover. This could be a win-win for both of them. To seal the deal and show good faith on Le Chen's part, he brought forth a transfer of ownership paper. The only question was the name to put down for the new owner. They looked at each other for a moment. Clint then suggested that the title could be held in the name of the Bronze Warrior Company. Chen broke out in an uncharacteristic laugh, but quickly brought himself under control. Chen agreed that the only people that used that term were the Chinese workers that had been saved by Charles Martinez. That title would immediately gain support from hundreds of Chinese workers in this region. Chen was sure that the non-Chinese in California had never heard the term nor would they have any idea what it meant if it were to come up.

Clint would retreat to his own cabin and mining shaft with title in hand. Le Chen would send up some guards to alert the cabin if any of the Starr Ranch group decided to check out that particular old cabin again. The word was around town that the lead man for the Starr Ranch cattle trading business had been killed over near Bay Town. Along with that loss and the killing of the two top gun-carrying Starr Ranch gamblers in Creston, the Starr Ranch men had grown nervous and were moving cautiously.

This shift in the attitude of the local Starr Ranch men allowed Clint to return to Creston for fun and food. It put him in close contact with Le Chen and their plan. Clint had to be trained to drive a freight wagon with two and three teams. Two weeks of practice and all agreed that Clint should drive one of the lighter wagons with a single team of horses. A lightweight fast wagon was put together so that it looked like a heavy freight wagon. Four cross-trained horses were selected. They demonstrated their pulling skills as well as their speed as saddle horses.

Chapter 15

Le Chen finally got the message that he had been anxiously waiting to hear. The next ship out of Hong Kong that would be carrying Chen's supplies would arrive at the end of the month. The cargo would have an escort of Quinn people that would only turn the shipment over to a direct representative of Le Chen. The ship was scheduled to arrive the last day of June if all sailing went as predicted. A payment of gold was required at the time of transfer.

Clint's training as a teamster was somewhat successful. The shooting skills that Clint was trying to develop in his newly formed Chinese gang were also somewhat productive. A group of 20 people had been assembled for the trip to San Francisco. Clint was dressed as one of the Asian guards and wagon drivers. Clint was given some make-up for his eyes and skin to help him blend into the gang. There was considerable joking among the group about his Chinese look. It was all good-natured and the Chinese men were very respectful since they had seen some of Clint's shooting skills during the preparation for this mission.

The caravan to San Francisco was a legitimate haul of supplies and payroll for the Chen warehouses and the arriving ship from Hong Kong. Every man knew the importance of the mission and the risks. This group was completely loyal to Le Chen and dedicated to his operation. Most of these men had benefited directly from the Le Chen trade between China, their homeland, and California. Not only had their lives been made much better, but most of their families back in China had received some help. Many of these men had already gotten some of their brothers and/or sisters out of desperate situations in China and into well-paying, safe jobs under Le Chen's wings.

The trip to San Francisco went without any problems. They were a week ahead of the scheduled arrival of the shipment from Hong Kong. This time was used to fully investigate the docks. Alternate escape routes were identified. The group of 20 split into small bands of four so as not to bring attention to themselves. Clint and his three mates kept close to the Chen warehouse. This was a big sacrifice for Clint. He knew some of the best gambling houses and cafés in San Francisco. The memory of his good old days in this bustling city hounded him every night. The Le Chen warehouse was on the edge of San Francisco's Chinatown and only a few blocks from the docks.

The most troubling news they heard was about the increase in looting and highway robbery as shipments left the docks. There had been a holdup of two freight wagons just one block from Chen's warehouse, making it clear that the thieves must be getting intelligence from dock people. The shipments that were being targeted were high value loads. Someone was alerting the bandits as to the contents of these shipments.

The Le Chen shipment would be a very high value cargo. Clint had slipped out a couple of times at night to look over the reported previous robbery sites. There was not a single route away from the docks that did not lead through at least one of these hazardous sections. The streets were narrow with multi-story buildings on both sides at some points. It was at these pinch points where most ambushes had occurred.

Clint had put together a plan that all 20 of his group went over. Some of the men were very familiar with the streets and neighborhoods. After a few alterations in the route, the group reached a consensus. The other parts of the plan required some imagination and artistry. The three heavy freight wagons and the light weight wagon were outfitted with some cotton bales. A slot was cut in the front of each wagon just under the driver's seat. The leather reins were fed through the slots so the driver could control the horses from a hiding place behind and below the seat. A small platform was built to hold the cotton bales above the wagon floor. Enough room was left for two people lying on their bellies to see out and drive the horses. The final touch was the making and decorating of two Chinese teamster dummies. The design had to accommodate real people driving the wagons when they left the docks, but be easily converted to safety wagons on the move. The group had discussed bringing the wagons to the Chen warehouse for conversion. The risk of someone learning of the disguise was more than the group wanted to take.

Their manpower would allocate three men per wagon. This would use 12 of the 20 on the four wagons. This would leave eight men on horses to ride escort. Clint was not sure how many people would be accompanying the young lady, Wan Quinn.

They would take six wagons to the docks for loading. Two wagons would take the heaviest cargo directly to the Chen Warehouse. A slower pace would be set by the four wagons destined for Creston. This would allow the two heavily loaded wagons time to reach the warehouse and be traded for mounts. These riders could bring up the rear and catch any ambushers in a cross-fire if there was an attack.

Clint had set one more safety precaution in his transportation plan. There were two high risk stretches on the chosen route according to Clint's calculations. Two snipers would be sent ahead to post one at the far end of each dangerous strip. They would hide in the shadows with rifles ready. Clint was not pleased with their marksmen skills. He had tried to improve their shooting but there had not been enough time. The men were eager students, but skill development took many hours and months of practice. The men were brave and knew the risk they would face once the shooting started.

Le Chen had ten men at the warehouse that wanted to return to China. People that were traveling with Wan Quinn that wanted to stay in California could be accommodated up to a total of ten. The shipping vouchers and travel permits had to match to avoid suspicions.

The ship arrived two days late but no difficulties had been experienced on the voyage. Le Chen's shipment to China had been checked-in at the shipping docks three days before the ship arrived. A constant rotation of Chen guards and dock helpers watched over the supplies around the clock. Chen's warehouse master had agreed with Clint that there were spies on the docks. The constant rotation of many Le Chen workers helped to set the stage for switching some crew members during the loading and unloading circus.

Even to Clint's good eyes for subtle details he did not pick up on the gender of the two small deck hands that slipped into his lightweight wagon. The space under the cotton bales was designed for two people. When Clint seated himself on the front seat he could tell that there was still plenty of room for him even with the two small bodies that lay on the wagon floor behind him. The loading was completed and an extra guard took up a position on the back of each wagon. The four wagons would move slowly to allow time for the riders from the warehouse to catch up.

The six freight wagons pulled out of the shipping docks under cover of darkness in a long slow line. As they passed the street entrance to the Chen Warehouse, the two heavily loaded lead wagons turned down the street to the warehouse. Those wagons were carrying seven new immigrants to California. His wagon had Wan Quinn and another small-frame body. It could be either a boy or girl; neither stowaway had shown their face. The slow-moving freight wagons were approaching the first bottleneck or hazard point. All four wagon drivers and guards slipped down under the cotton bales and moved the dummies into position. The men that had taken the two extra wagons to the warehouse had not caught up to the rear yet.

The passage through the first pinch point went slowly. It was hard to see and control the horses from under the seat. The pace was too slow. It would give any ambushers and snipers too much time to look over the set up. Clint picked up the speed a little. The three wagons behind him were right close. The guard riders were spaced out in front and between each wagon. Clint could feel his heart pounding and sweat was getting into his eyes. The next potential highjacking stretch was coming up in a few blocks.

The wagons were walled-in on both sides at this street section with three-story buildings. The four wagons were in the middle of the constricted section when a hail of bullets suddenly rained down on them. The snipers were on the rooftops on both sides of the street. Clint saw dust puff out of the dummy on his seat. One guard rider up in front of his team went down. The horses were given a hard slap with the lines and they lurched forward to escape the gunfire. Clint felt a hot burning in his side. He had slid too far forward so he could control the horses. A second slug came through the wagon seat and sliced his left arm and shoulder.

Rifle fire was coming from a corner building offset up in front of his team. The flame of the gun was pointed up toward the rooftops. His man was shooting at the rooftop snipers. The sound of horses coming up the street behind them was very close. The guard on the back of his wagon had been firing up toward the rooftops. The rifle fire was now directed back down the street toward the approaching horses from the rear. It was no more than seconds but it seemed like an hour before a gunfight broke out between Chen's men and the riders behind the wagons. The warehouse reinforcements had finally caught up.

Clint then abandoned his hiding position under the seat and with deadly aim dropped two snipers off the rooftop on one side and another one on the other side. This firepower broke the will of the ambushers. The remaining horsemen behind the wagons escaped down an alley with Chen's men sending lead after them. Chen's riders gathered around the wagons and helped load the three wounded and two dead guards. With every one mounted or riding in the wagons, they headed out as fast as the narrow street would allow.

Chapter 16

The soft delightful sounds of female voices came to Clint's foggy head. The words were not English but sounded sweet in this dreamlike state. His eyes did not seem to open on command. His body felt like a huge burden was lying on his chest. Breath was hard to draw in and his rib cage hurt something awful. His arms and legs felt too heavy to lift. The dream continued into almost a nightmare. Was he still alive? The pain told him that indeed this was real life. A little more concentration and the eyelids parted just enough to let in some light.

It seemed like hours, but the lapse of time was probably only minutes. The first image to come to his mind was the beautiful face of a young Chinese woman. He was not sure if it was real or a dream. A smooth soft voice was flowing from the crimson red lips of the Oriental face. It took a little while for Clint to realize the young Chinese lady was talking to him in excellent English. Her voice was clear and presented perfect words that Clint's mind was starting to comprehend. He tried to raise one of his arms, but it seemed to be paralyzed.

He then opened his eyes wide and that action caused a stir in the room. People were chattering in Chinese. One or two people were moving around the room. He heard a door open and close. Bright colored clothes were moving around his body. A soft hand covered his forehead and cheek. A damp cool cloth was also wiping his face. The coolness of the cloth made Clint realize he was burning up with fever. The dampness of the sheets told him that he had gone through a fever sweat.

Three oval faces with dark eyes and stacks of black hair on top were peering down on him. The faces were without a flaw. Two of the faces were of young ladies not more than 18 years old. The other lady was just as pretty, but was ten to 15 years older and a little thinner. None of the three were very tall and probably weighed less than one hundred pounds each. He was beginning to think he had died and gone to a paradise full of gorgeous women. The spell was broken by another door noise and the face of Le Chen scattered the oval faces.

The face of Le Chen brought Clint's mind back to earth. Chen explained that he was not paralyzed... only tied down so his wound wouldn't open up again. He had lost a lot of blood and one side of his lung had been pierced. A bamboo tube was draining the fluid so he could breathe. He would heal fine under the able care of Chan Quinn, a cousin of his bride. Her kind face appeared beside Le Chen. It was the oldest of the three beautiful faces that had been staring down at him. A few more comforting words and Le Chen took the hand of the prettiest of the three ladies. She was introduced as Wan Quinn, his bride, the lady that had ridden on the wagon floor beside Clint during the escape out of San Francisco's back streets. The looks between Le Chen and Wan Quinn told Clint that they both were pleased with their decisions. He and Wan excused themselves leaving Clint in the hands of two beautiful women. He really did think that the land of paradise had found him. The soft touch of their hands almost made the pain go away.

Within three more days, Clint was up and walking with the help of these two ladies. He really could walk on his own, but why fight the system? The bamboo pipe had been removed and his side was healing rapidly with the help of some bad-smelling creams. He was ready for some strong coffee but tea was the drink he was offered. His other wound looked pretty raw. A bullet had torn a wide gash in his shoulder muscle but no bones were damaged. Some very neat stitches ran across the long deep red zone on his shoulder. Wan Quinn, the medical person in this group, insisted that his left arm be tied to his waistband for two weeks. She felt the muscle could knit itself together if great care was taken and the arm was held immobile. The attention and care was so nice that Clint easily settled into the life of being cared-for. It was tough, but he would try to endure. This type of thinking almost made him chuckle. Then the thought of laughing with these painful ribs and chest cleared his head.

Clint received an update from Le Chen almost every day. Chen's men were watching the movements of the Starr Ranch personnel. Things had become very quiet after the San Francisco gun battle and rescue of Wan Quinn. Two of Chen's men had been killed in the escape and three wounded. All three of the wounded were recovering without permanent damage. The gossip out of San Francisco was that the Phillips Freight Company and the Starr Ranch had lost seven men on the raid.

Le Chen had continued the surveillance on Starr Ranch personnel with some interesting findings. The two gold robberies had put a real financial crimp in the operations. The gossip around the cafés and bathhouses that Chen ran in Sacramento suggested that the Starr Ranch men had run off the old hunchback gambler from Creston. They bragged that they had put the fear into him. He most likely left the country for good. The other rumor was that a phantom rider had ambushed some of their men. It was probably the same bandit that stole the gold in Creston. It would not surprise Mr. Starr to learn that the same mystery gunman was involved in the gold shipment loss outside of Sacramento. The Starr Ranch had hired the Pinkerton National Detective Agency to track down this mystery bandit and all the lost gold. Le Chen was not sure, but he thought the business-looking man that often sat in the poker games in Creston was a Pinkerton agent.

Along with the rumors about Phillips Freight and Starr Ranch, Clint heard numerous details about the Le Chen and Wan Quinn wedding. The young Chinese nurses taking care of Clint each told him their tale on the wedding and three-day feast. Sprinkled throughout the tale were frequent thanks for getting Wan Quinn through that terrible gauntlet of bad men. The wedding and feast had occurred three days after her safe arrival but while Clint was heavily sedated to let his wounds heal without motion.

A couple of the Chinese guards Clint had helped train also came by with thanks. A third man in his mid-twenties introduced himself as Tow Quinn, Wan Quinn's brother. His appreciation of Clint's help in providing safe passage for his sister was heartfelt. He also pledged himself to provide whatever help Clint needed. He had survived three years in the Chinese

Army and providing protection for the Quinn family had been his job for the past five years. He was asked by his and Wan Quinn's father to accompany Wan to America. Le Chen had already given him the task of guarding Clint's mining cabin and horses. Tow Quinn was eager to take on Clint's enemies as proof of his thanks and loyalty.

Clint immediately felt that he had a capable and reliable partner in Tow Quinn. In the presence of Le Chen, Clint laid out his mission and need for the phantom rider cover. Clint could see the intrigue in Tow's eyes as he took on Clint's feeling of rage toward the Starr Ranch. Le Chen insisted that Clint needed at least six or seven weeks of rest and physical therapy. Tow Quinn would ride the circuits of Chen's stores and cafés to find a way to do major harm to the Starr Ranch. The goal was to convince the Starr Ranch people to never threaten the two Bay Town ranches again.

The first month of confinement was difficult for Clint. The release of the bonds to his recovery room opened up his spirits. He was able to take on the teaching role for a small army of Chinese guards. Tow Quinn was an able leader and quick to refine his rifle and handgun skills. His three years in the Chinese Army had been mostly police duty. His group patrolled streets, controlled crowds and collected taxes. The Chinese Army had only limited modern weapons. They did not train the masses of young soldiers in weaponry. Tow Quinn was well-suited for surveillance, spying and undercover work. He had the skills to blend into the service sector that Le Chen operated all along the coast from San Francisco to Sacramento. Information on the Phillips Freight and Starr Ranch personnel was reported daily. Clint probably knew more about the Starr Ranch men than the company did. The customers at the cafés, bathhouses and stores paid little attention to the Chinese help. Most of the customers did not even realize that nearly all of Chen's people understood and spoke excellent English. The customers dealt with Chen's personnel as if they didn't exist. They freely talked about their boss, the work they were assigned and any other gossip that came to their minds.

Tow Quinn frequently moved through the various places as the hired help. No one paid any attention to another Chinese helper. This gave Tow firsthand information on the workings of the Starr Ranch. He was able to identify their best gunmen. Tracking any new men was critical, especially if new successful gunslingers were being hired. The schedules of drug shipments and payments were not that difficult to determine. To come up with a plan to hurt the Starr Ranch, but keeping Le Chen's undercover operation safe, was the challenge.

Tow Quinn came up with a scheme but it was too brutal even for Clint. A Chinese gang back in his home province had poisoned the cocaine that a rival drug gang was selling. Hundreds of Chinese users had died, but it wiped out the competition. Their drugs were not trusted so no one would buy from them. Tow recollected that the tainted drug gang left the area within months of the widespread poisoning. The citizens ganged-up on a lot of the drug dealers and clubbed them to death. Tow thought there was some justice in the whole thing because many of the dead drug users were scum, robbers and thieves. Le Chen and Clint were sure a better plan could be found.

Chapter 17

Clint was feeling his old self again. The shoulder muscle was healing just like Chan Quinn had predicted. He was on a muscle building program prescribed by the two beautiful nurses that watched him like a hawk. They were sweet, but could be ruthless if he stepped out of line on the program. Chan Quinn was proud of her medical skills. She did not want a show-off cowboy to undo her work.

The training of the Chinese guards was progressing well ahead of Clint's expectations. The large American handguns were not easy for the smaller hands of his men. Le Chen came up with the idea that the smaller caliber handgun could be used instead of the customary .44 caliber revolver that most of the American gunslingers were using. The .35 caliber slug would not have the knock down power of the larger .44 caliber, but it would kill. Le Chen had obtained a shipment of .35 caliber pistols that had been destined for Singapore. Clint did not want to know any more about that transaction. Le Chen set up a retooling shop in the back of his blacksmith operation. A top quality gunsmith was located with experience at a Colt factory back east. The adaptation was done with ease. The hand grips were sized for each man.

The smaller caliber pistols were fitted with slightly longer barrels and thus their accuracy was equal to the standard long barrel .44 caliber handgun. The lighter weight and smaller grip proved the winning ticket for his men. Most of Le Chen's recruits were well schooled in hand-to-hand combat. The men were also skilled at knife and sword fighting. However, the American west style of fighting didn't use close contact engagement. The western man was more apt to shoot you first and then walk up to see who he had killed. The oriental close-combat fighter never got the chance to prove his superior skills. The one place his Chinese guards proved to be very effective was in urban, back-street business protection. Anyone that did harm to Le Chen's people could disappear without a trace. A Chinese court was run behind the scenes. Grievances between the Asian people were settled in this court. Cases against outside people were presented to a senior panel. The verdicts came down and the sentences were given to the elite guards for execution. All of this activity was done outside the local law. Very little attention was given to the Chinese from the American law enforcement organizations. The Chinese system of justice was completely out-of-mind and sight of the general population. Le Chen worked hard to keep the system secret.

Time had passed rapidly for Clint. The attention of pretty young women was no doubt a contributing factor. He had gotten so involved in training the Chen company guards that he hardly realized his recovery was almost complete. It was time for him to move out of the comfort of Chen's care and back into the real world. Tow Quinn reported regularly on Clint's cabin and mining location. There had not been any return visits from the Starr Ranch riders. Clint would move back to his own shack and its solitude. He knew the comforting care would be missed, but his mission was weighing heavy on his mind.

Another driving force developed as he watched the happiness of Le Chen and Wan Quinn. The young couple was busy planning their future and working toward a common goal. A void was felt in Clint's heart as he saw the sharing of love between these two people. He wanted to finish his job of saving the two ranches for the two ex-Army couples, then get on with his own life. Besides, he had no idea what was happening to his brother back in New Mexico territory.

Clint's daily exercise and firearms practice was showing good results. He was back to near his full strength and skill level when an interesting tidbit of information arrived. The Le Chen workers in a Sacramento gambling house passed the word that the old hunched back trail bum that had been run out of Creston was playing poker again. The Starr Ranch men along with some Pinkerton agents had tracked the man to an old mining camp up in the mountains. They were watching his movements hoping to find the big gold catch that was taken out of the Creston poker games. Clint felt guilt bear down on himself. This old miner and trail bum probably had no idea that he might be punished for Clint's misdeeds. Time was pressing Clint into action if he was going to save this old man. He could not sit idly by and let another be punished for his mischief.

Le Chen had made arrangements to transfer all of Clint's gold to a Santa Fe bank with which

Clint had a working arrangement. A few other details were worked out and Clint hit the trail with all his horses and firepower. Le Chen wanted to have a big farewell feast, but Clint begged off. Le Chen insisted that Tow Quinn and a half dozen of the best guards go with Clint to Sacramento. Le Chen made the point that Clint could do the final training of the men in a real field exercise. It was a face-saving gesture on both their parts. Clint knew that Le Chen was fully aware that his men were already highly trained and skilled in the trade. Clint graciously accepted the offer.

The initiated plan was to rescue the old miner from the trap that he had unknowingly walked into. A second part was to inflict as much damage to the Starr Ranch and Phillips Freight Company as possible. It was hoped that one more major blow would deter any further attacks and harassment of his two Bay Town ranches. The details of the plan had to be carefully worked out. Clint wanted to keep his identity secret, but the Starr Ranch owners must identify the connection between their pain and the safety of the Bay Town ranches.

Clint had taken on the Oriental look as best as he could. The group of seven Chinese gunmen looked a little odd in the western California coastal area. Most Chinese workers kept their peasant-looking dress along with their pigtails. The general public paid them almost no attention, and considered them almost as part of the background. The shock of seeing seven heavily armed Chinese men in western clothing with holsters and handguns was confusing. It was so unreal that most of the people could not identify a single one of those riders separately. This was the hope. All seven rode their way straight into town and into one of the stables that served Le Chen's bathhouses, cafés and laundry services. This allowed Clint to get his firepower into place.

The visual transformation of those six Chinese gunmen back to lowly servants was done in minutes. Clint stayed under cover as his six men moved through the gambling halls to locate the old man. It took two days before the old man was spotted. Tow Quinn's men were excellent servants as they blended into the background of the target saloon. Identifying the Starr Ranch and Phillips Freight people was not hard. The uncertain part was putting a label on the Pinkerton agents. A sketch artist was put to work drawing each man that Tow Quinn selected. It should not have surprised Clint, but he did get a little jump in his heartbeat when the businessman/gambler from Creston showed up among the sketches.

Le Chen's spies had reported that the old man's pattern was five days of gambling and good eating and then he would disappear for a week or two. This should give enough time to identify the other Pinkerton agents now that one had been spotted. The old man had a room in the back of Le Chen's laundry building. It was a cheap flophouse with half a dozen rooms and no service. Most of the occupants were down-and-out miners and trail bums. They got one free bath per week with the room. That extra benefit was more for the landlord than the tenant.

The number of gunmen and Pinkerton agents watching the old man was about nine, give or take a couple. Tow Quinn and Clint agreed on the identity of two Pinkerton agents in addition to the businessman. The Phillips Freight Company had two men that appeared to be paying close attention to the old man gambler. Then there were at least three tough-looking gunmen from the Starr Ranch operations.

Chen's people that worked all kinds of support jobs around the gambling saloon fed the whispered conversations back to Quinn and Clint. It was fairly easy to piece together the planning and assignments as they developed. Even the Pinkerton agents didn't seem to realize that the Chinese workers had ears and were able to understand English. The plan that seemed to be approved by the head Pinkerton agent and the lead Starr Ranch boss was an ambush. The Pinkerton agent with displayed badge would confront the old man and accuse him of stealing gold coins from the Starr Ranch. This would spook the old man and cause him to flee Sacramento. An ambush would be set up on the last fork of the main road where the old man had previously turned off to his cabin. The two men that had been watching the cabin would be in hiding as the group from the saloon would drive the old man to them. The plan would be quick and deadly. The old man's gold was most likely hidden in or near his shack. Once the old fellow was dead, they could tear the cabin apart and recover the lost Starr Ranch gold.

Clint was hoping that Tow Quinn's men hidden up at the old man's hideout could disable the Starr Ranch watchdogs. This had to be done without alerting the other group that would be chasing the old man. Tow assured Clint that his men were skilled with knife and sword in the dark of night. Four of the Chinese warriors were sent to line the road between the fork in the main road and the cabin.

The challenge by the Pinkerton officer came almost too soon. Tow's men had just left the stables headed out toward the old man's hidden cabin when the Starr plan went into action. The old man was as rattled as the Starr plan had hoped. He scurried to his room and packed his belongings in a panic. He was in the Chen's stable packing his mule and horse when he collapsed. The stable helper sought out Tow Quinn to report the problem. The examination of the man found him to be dead. The fear had caused him to have a heart attack and die.

Clint's mind was reeling. He had come to Sacramento to rescue this man. Now he lay dead on the floor of the stable. A look through his dirty clothes proved that this old man was just a poor, broke, old, has-been miner with a crooked back. It was just bad luck that the Starr Ranch and the Pinkertons had mistakenly identified him as the gambler from Creston. While looking down on the dirty, crumpled body, a thought came to Clint. Tow Quinn liked it. Tow offered to be the decoy. He had great riding skills and was the best shot of the Chinese warriors. Clint thought it was too great a risk. One reason was that the four Chinese men had already left to guard the trail. They would not know that Tow was impersonating the old man. Clint gave into his own version of the plan, but with many second thoughts about risking the head of the Chinese warriors.

Clint's version of the plan included the body of the old man. The old man's body was packed onto the mule instead of the supplies. The bundle looked the same when securely tied. Tow Quinn pulled the old man's clothes and hat on with firm hands, but a turned up nose. Just before Tow bolted out the stable doors in a dead run with the difficult mule on a long rope, Clint reminded him that one Starr Ranch man must survive and inspect the old man's dead body. With those words, the scheme was set into motion.

Clint and the only remaining Chinese warrior waited for Tow Quinn and baggage to clear town. They then slowly moved out of the stable. The sound of half a dozen riders was heard up ahead. He had to slow the warrior beside him to make sure the Starr riders and the Pinkertons did not suspect that anyone was on their trail. The illusion that the Starr men were the hunters rather than the prey had to be maintained until they reached the main road turnoff. The real risk was that some over-eager rider would try to gun-down the old man before he turned into the wooded lane and its dark protection. Clint was betting Tow's life on the discipline that the Pinkertons held on their riders.

The partial moonlight gave Clint a long distance view as they crested a large hill about ten miles out of Sacramento. Clint and his men were a good mile behind the Starr riders, who were within a quarter mile of the slow-moving mule. The spyglass brought Tow Quinn's dilemma up close. Clint waved his partner over into some trees out of sight. He then shot two times into the air. The Starr riders slowed as Clint had hoped. They even pulled up and milled around a little. Clint could guess they were trying to decide if someone was behind them or if these were just random shots in the night. After a few minutes, the group headed after the old man again, but one rider was left trailing the pack as a rear guard lookout. This was typical military strategy that Clint was banking on. The Pinkertons were mostly ex-military men that liked hunting and arresting or killing other men.

Clint and his one man stayed back under cover, but tried to keep the same distance between themselves and the rear lookout. Hope was all they could offer Tow Quinn. Luck had to be on their side if this scheme had any chance of success. Tow's upfront men had to disable the ambush in waiting but not alert the gang chasing Tow. If all went as planned, Tow would lead the mule with the dead body right into his own men. This all depended on all four Chinese warriors getting into place before the Starr gang came barreling up the road with guns a'blazing.

The gunfire that erupted up in the forest a good mile and a half from Clint was rapid and sustained for only a few minutes. The stillness of the night then followed the rush of gun shots. In most battles, single shots will continue for some time after the primary attack. This time there was only complete silence.

Clint moved up close under the sounds of the battle. The Starr rear guard had sped toward the battle forgetting his important rear lookout assignment. In contrast, with spyglass scanning the road and forest up ahead, Clint and his man held their positions. He reminded his sidekick that one man needed to be allowed to pass. Finally two horses broke free of the forest cover. The first horse and rider was the rear lookout. He was leading another horse with a badly wounded man trying to hold on. Clint signaled to his man to stay under cover and allow the two horses to pass. When the dust finally settled on the moonlit road, they came out of their hiding place. It was a good 20-minute ride before they came upon the ambush site. There slumped against a giant redwood tree was the old man. Clint and his aide got down to examine the bodies. Tow Quinn and all his men appeared out of the darkness of the forest. The moonlight was coming through the giant tree tops in little spots. There was just enough light to make out the old man's body fully dressed in his old clothes, but full of bullet holes. The other dead bodies were in a close cluster back down the road not more than 50 yards away. Tow's men checked all the bodies to make sure all were dead.

The pre-planned arrangement of the bodies did not take long. The bodies of the two front guards that Starr had sent on ahead were dragged down and placed up the road from the old man's body. Clint took a handful of golden eagle coins out of his saddlebags and loaded the old man's pockets.

Quinn had a couple of his men take a handful of coins up to the old man's cabin and hide them in various places. Then everyone spread out to cover all their tracks and any sign of their role in the ambush.

Chapter 18

With a rider out in front, the Chinese warriors went back to Creston and Le Chen's establishment. One chore was left to complete the ambush. Clint had composed a letter from the Bronze Warrior to the old man. It thanked him for his work in stripping money from the Starr Ranch and Phillips Freight Company. The letter promised any additional help he would need to deter the raids against the two ranches that the late Charles Martinez had deeded to the two ex-Army soldiers and their families. It was signed by the Bronze Warrior. One of Le Chen's staff had done an excellent job of using Old English lettering to compose the letter.

The letter was then sent up to the old man's cabin to be hidden, but not too well. The two riders that took the letter were cautioned to be discreet. Clint was sure the Pinkertons would be investigating this whole incident. If the cabin had already been ransacked, then hiding the letter would be more difficult.

For the next two days, Clint worked on his gear preparing for his trip back to Santa Fe. His horses were in great shape and ready for the long trip. Le Chen had approached Clint saying that four of his men wanted to travel to Durango. They had family out there in the silver mines north of Durango. Chinese riders traveling alone were often harassed or even killed by western hoodlums. Chen had high respect for Clint's skills as a fighter and traveler. It would be a lot safer for these men to travel with an experienced western trail man. Le Chen suggested that Clint would have a chance to continue his training with Chinese sword and knife. One of these men who had friends and family in Durango was a topnotch swordsman. The suggestion was that Clint could continue training the Chinese men in western firearms, and they could train him in the art of sword-fighting and back-alley knife skills.

This discussion was called short when the two men returned with the letter. The Pinkerton agents were at the old man's cabin when they got there. They stayed clear so no one would know of their presence. They reported that the old man's body and all the others had been removed, most likely taken back to Sacramento. The lead Pinkerton was the businessman that had played poker with Clint in Creston. Clint had hoped that the cool, controlled Pinkerton agent had met his fate during the ambush. The businessman-looking agent had apparently sent others to do the dirty work while he stayed in Sacramento. If that businessman looked closely at the old man's face, he would most likely conclude that the Creston gambler and this dead old man were two different people. This could unravel the plan that Clint had so carefully constructed.

Clint set out for Sacramento with all his horses, an ample supply of gold and a dozen young warriors. Le Chen had sent the bulk of his gold coins to the Santa Fe banker as the two of them had agreed. The number of young Chinese men that wanted to make the trip east to Durango had grown to eight. Four of the dozen heavily-armed Chinese men would stay in Sacramento. Clint had the fleeting sensation of an Asian chieftain leading his army into battle. The whole group was dressed in western clothes with bandanas and wide-brim cowboy hats. A close look could discern the oriental features, even with the makeup and dirty clothes. A couple of Le Chen's helpers had spent considerable time making up Clint's face using a skin plaster that gave an older look, and added aging lines painted on his face.

The letter that had been so artfully crafted was still in Clint's possession. The idea of the letter was a viable plan but only if it could be discovered by the right people. Four men were sent back to the old man's cabin to retrieve any artifacts of his past. They were to look for photos, legal papers, keepsakes, small tools and some old clothes. If any type of carrying case was in the cabin, they were instructed to bring all the items to the Le Chen stables in Sacramento.

Arriving in the outskirts of Sacramento, everyone split up and worked their way to the stables separately. The early evening was just setting in on the town and the alleyways that the men moved through had grown very black. Only the flickering of lanterns in windows and doorways gave a dim light to navigate the dark back-streets. It took the group of riders over an hour for the last one to reach the safety of the stable.

Two very pretty Chinese saloon waitresses had just returned to Le Chen's boarding rooms that were in a building between the stables and the laundry facility. Their job had been to track the businessman gambler that Clint was sure was the lead Pinkerton agent. They had one hour off before their next duty time. Tow Quinn and Clint talked to the two young ladies to learn all they could about the Pinkerton man, who was a shrewd poker player, as Clint already knew. There were three saloons that he frequented each night. His pattern was to select a back table with equal distances to the front and rear exits. He was patient as demonstrated by the long wait time he would invest just to get the right seat. His rotation between saloons appeared random, so there was not any way to predict which poker game he would enter next.

The entire gang of 12 warriors donned the dress of café and saloon helpers. They spread themselves among the three gaming rooms that the waitresses had pointed out. Clint was the exception to the Asian worker appearance. He put on the Mexican appearance of a wealthy gambler with plenty of gold. Facial makeup put his age at mid- to late-50s.

Rather than try to predict which poker table the Pinkerton agent would select, Clint made a choice. He carefully selected a back corner poker table with this chair against the wall. The saloon mirrors gave him almost a complete view in all directions. One of Le Chen's barmaids told Clint that the Pinkerton man often sat at that very seat. The same barmaid would deliver plenty of drinks with her special touch.

It did not take long for Clint's superior gambling skills to attract attention. The growing pile of chips in front of this well-dressed Mexican gambler spoke volumes to the nearby customers. The first break in play came after only two hours of steady poker. The dealer took his restroom break and new players joined the table. Good poker players love a challenge so it was not surprising that two or three of the best in the place replaced the losers. Clint did a good job of impressing these new players. His consistent winning of a few big pots got their attention as well as that of the onlookers.

The second round of games was almost over when Clint finally spotted the Pinkerton man. He moved with caution and fluid motion along the bar until he found a good vantage point. Even though the eyes of the dealer and the agent met for only a split second, Clint caught the connection. The inner smile that Clint felt never reached any outward display. A confrontation was very close.

The players returned after the second break. It was no surprise that the Pinkerton agent was seated directly across the table from Clint. Several of the second round players did not return. This new table group was definitely more serious and sinister than the first two rounds. Clint's skill in reading people told him that this could be big, deadly trouble. He let the first few rounds go by without a challenge. The man to his left was bluffing a lot but Clint let it work. The fourth time that Clint folded his cards, yielding to a bluff, his eyes were looking straight into the piercing eyes of the Pinkerton agent. There was no doubt in Clint's mind that the Pinkerton man was sure this fancy Mexican gambler was the old hunched-back gambler from Creston. Anyone looking on would never suspect the boiling energy below these two cool faces.

The tense spell between the two men was broken by the local lawman coming to the table. He excused himself and whispered something into the Pinkerton man's ear. The dealer asked if a break needed to be called. Most of the players nodded in agreement and the table took a break. The Pinkerton man left the saloon with the lawman and two others.

The barmaid that had been taking care of Clint slipped him a note. Tow Quinn had been able to retrieve some of the old man's belongings. A bag of his stuff along with the letter had been turned over to one of the local deputies. His room was being cleaned out and the bag was found by one of the cleaning ladies. This was the reason the Pinkerton agent was called out of the poker game. Clint disposed of the note from Tow and then chose a good position at the bar. A round of free drinks brought a group to gather around Clint. Free liquor had a way of giving you friends that you never suspected. A good time was being had by all when the serious-looking Pinkerton agent returned to the saloon. The crowd soon sensed the tension in the air and moved away from Clint and the bar area.

Their eyes locked and Clint knew the time had come. His grand scheme had not fooled this sharp businessman. No doubt the agent was confident of his own skills. The man sounded out in an authoritative voice that Clint should meet him at the local Sheriff's office. A number of questions had arisen about the recent death of an old man. The agent was sure that Clint might have some background information on the old man. A shipment of gold coins had been stolen from the Starr Ranch. Some of the money recovered from the old man's pack bag was from the stolen shipment. The agent was interested in the source of this fancy Mexican gambler's gold coins. The crowd was told that this was only an investigation. This whole thing could most likely be cleared up at the Sheriff's office.

Chapter 19

Clint was given two escorts to help him get his belongings from his room. There was no doubt in Clint's mind that this would be his last trip anywhere. He fumbled around his room as long as the two deputies would allow. A good sized pouch of gold coins was collected by one of the deputies. It did not take much insight to tell that Clint was headed toward an accidental death. The two guards escorted Clint out the back door of the rooming house. He was directed to follow the alley down two blocks and then turn left up the side street. The lantern lights from the main street up ahead just about blinded Clint as he looked from the dark side street into the street lamps. The sound behind him indicated that the two deputies had spread out. Clint was no fool. Their move behind him took these rear guards out of the line of fire that would surely come from the street up ahead.

He was about halfway up the dark street when a silhouette of a man appeared at the entrance. It was not hard to guess that the Pinkerton man was the figure standing with the light behind him. Even if he could drop the main man, which Clint was not confident about, the two men behind him would fill him full of lead. There really wasn't a choice because Clint was sure they planned on killing him right here in this dark, dusty side street. The Pinkerton agent had given enough accusing information back at the saloon to set the stage for his attempted escape. The gold coins would be turned in to the sheriff as evidence of his connection to the Starr Ranch robberies. Clint would be no more than a footnote in the Sacramento newspaper. The sheriff and the Pinkerton agents had solved the gold shipment thefts from the Phillips Freight Company and the Starr Ranch.

Clint moved a slight bit to his left so that one of the street lanterns was directly behind the Pinkerton agent. He had kept his steady pace toward the agent and this may have given Clint a little edge. This distance was less than 100 feet when a small tilt of the agent's shoulder gave Clint all the signal he would get. His gun was in his hand in a flash. Two shots rang out of Clint's pistol before a single round ever left the agent's sidearm.

A spinning motion was Clint's only hope of missing the slugs that were surely coming toward his back. No sound was heard from the dusty street behind him. With the light behind Clint, he could see the slumped bodies of the two rear guard deputies. Rising up from the rear were two of his Chinese friends. A quick search of the two deputies recovered the gold sack. These two guards behind Clint had been stabbed with a sharp dagger. To mask this type of killing, both dead men were shot twice. The two Chinese men dissolved into the darkness taking most of the gold coins. They were told to drop a few coins along the back alley like a trail of cookie crumbs. Clint stuffed just a few in his pockets and lay down on the ground waiting for the arrival of on-lookers.

It was only minutes after the shooting stopped that the alley was full of people. The sheriff soon arrived and took charge. Clint was lifted up rather roughly and stood against the building. The sheriff took his firearm and smelled the barrel. There was enough street light for Clint to see the surprise on the sheriff's face.

He was hauled off to the jail for more questioning. Clint stuck to one story: He had been robbed of his gold sack and almost killed. He had dropped to the ground when the shooting started. It was too dark to see anyone. His surprisingly cool gun supported his statement that he had never fired a shot. The frustrated sheriff locked Clint up. After all, two deputies and the head Pinkerton agent had been killed. On top of those deaths, a sack of gold coins had been stolen from right under the protective plan of the sheriff. The Pinkerton agent had promised the sheriff proof of the people behind the Starr Ranch gold heists.

All he had now was a wealthy Mexican gambler that was suggesting the sheriff's office or the Pinkerton's had almost killed him and stole his money. This was a grand mess that the Pinkerton man had put the local sheriff squarely in the middle of. The sheriff refused to let Clint out of jail until more of his questions could be answered.

The midmorning sun was warming the streets outside the jail as well as Clint's cell. The sounds of voices seeped down the jail hall to Clint's ears. The sheriff's voice was now familiar to him. Another voice that Clint knew well was Le Chen's. It was not long before the sheriff, two deputies and three Chinese men came to his cell door. Le Chen in his best expressionless face stood silently beside the sheriff as the cell door was unbolted. The sheriff was almost apologetic in his tone to Clint as there were no charges, just a misunderstanding during all the problems of last night.

Le Chen asked the sheriff if the Mexican gambler could travel to Carson City. The gambler had paid Le Chen a good sum for protection and travel to the gambling casinos in Carson City. It was clear to the sheriff that this gambler was not a threat if he could not ride to Carson City alone without protection. Le Chen explained to everyone that his company was hauling linens, laundry supplies and workers to a nearby casino in Carson City where the silver strikes were roaring.

Clint played the humble part of a gutless but well-dressed gambler. He did not want to miss his chance at well-protected travel over the mountains to Carson City. He had heard that there were many holdups along that trail. The sheriff seemed glad to turn this gambler over to Le Chen's care and be done with him.

Chapter 20

It was midday when Le Chen led Clint into a well-appointed dining room, full with at least 20 guests. He was seated with honors at the head table beside Le Chen and his wife, Wan Quinn. The 12 warriors who had accompanied Clint on this last mission were seated along one side. The other half of the table held a dozen older Chinese gentlemen in traditional Chinese clothing. The 12 warriors were outfitted in Mexican outfits with lots of silver. Their uniforms almost matched the costume that Clint had been wearing as a Mexican gambler. The whole setting and was like a grand banquet.

Le Chen toasted Clint for a job well-done. He went into some detail how the entire operation had been planned by Clint. He then went into a long thank-you speech about Clint's able assistance in safely delivering his wife from the San Francisco ship. He would be forever indebted to Clint for making his life complete.

Tow Quinn then came around the table and handed Clint's revolvers to him. Clint thanked Tow for his quick thinking during the alley gun battle last night. The replacement handguns that Tow had switched with Clint's made his story hold water. If his handguns had been recently fired, Clint would probably still be in jail. A bow between these two admiring warriors brought a big cheer from the table. Even the elderly men along one side of the table let out an audible sound, even if subdued.

As a final tribute, Clint was approached by a dozen beautiful young ladies as they pecked his cheek with a kiss and placed a flower string around his neck.

Le Chen called the celebration to a close by wishing Clint happiness and safety on his journeys. The Chen house would always be open to him.

The wagons, horses and Mexican-looking soldiers all left Sacramento for Carson City. The Mexican gambler was riding high in his saddle atop a big bay horse. There was warmth in Clint's heart that the phantom rider had saved the two Bay Town ranches without bringing harm to his two ex-Army men and their families.

The trail back through Durango should be a great trip. In his company of eight Chinese warriors was one of the best Chinese chefs of San Francisco. Life on the trail was not meant to be so good.

The End

About the Author

William F. Martin was born on a Kentucky farm and moved west in the mid-sixties on an assignment with the federal government's program to help Native Americans. His assignment to Santa Fe, New Mexico, began a lifetime love affair with the American West. His writing interest was developed with the publishing of many technical journal articles and textbooks on environmental and engineering issues. He obtained a B.S. degree in Civil Engineering from the University of Kentucky and a M.S. degree in Environmental Engineering from the University of Texas.

After assignments in South Dakota, Arizona, and Texas, he has lived near the Gulf of Mexico on Treasure Island, Florida, and in the Blue Ridge Mountains in Boone, North Carolina.